Splatter

Jordonna | Bercy Jr. | Collins | Healy

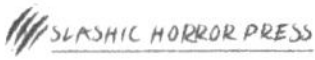
SLASHIC HORROR PRESS

Please note that a content notice can be found on the final page of this book.

Wonderland

The Past Never Dies

Wonderland

ANGELIQUE JORDONNA

ONE

"Welcome to my wonderland," Kyle whispered, a slight erotic rasp in her voice. Soft and elegant. She did not stutter. Kyle wanted the woman to know that this was her place of astonishment and awe—that she was the ruler of Wonderland.

Her whole being ached for the woman when Kyle spied a shiver passing through her body. Those four simple words always brought terror to anyone who heard them, and they brought Kyle so much joy. She felt a tingling in her stomach like a colony of little spiders were running amok inside that pit deep within her.

Welcome to my wonderland, her brain repeated over and over again. *Welcome. Welcome indeed. Bienvenue dans mon pays des merveilles. Benvenuti nel mio Paese delle Meraviglie.*

The thoughts got away from her and began taking on a life of their own. The words in Kyle's head rambled on and on and on and she had to force herself back to reality.

It made her smile though. She felt her lips curling up, sure she looked like a psychopath in the dimly lit room, but she didn't care. She was in her safe place, her land of happy. Nothing else mattered in Kyle's world right then.

Wonderland! Like the secret world Alice found when she fell down the rabbit hole. Except Kyle didn't have to fall down no damn hole. She just took a few steps down into the basement and it was a whole new world for her.

Every. Single. Time.

Kyle's eyes glanced back at the woman in front of her and she couldn't help but want her in so many ways. She wanted to touch her soft flesh and show her just how much she appreciated her. *How much she should appreciate me,* she thought. *I want to press my lips tightly against hers, feel the warmth of her body next to mine. Just some kind of physical contact, anything at all. I need it.*

She struggled for a mere second, stopping once the razor-sharp barbed wire pierced her flesh. Little droplets of blood formed and slowly dripped from the wounds. Kyle imagined she could hear the sound as one compact droplet hit the ground beneath her. Just a miniature splash that echoed in her head and made her dizzy with lust.

She took in a deep breath, her fear giving off an intoxicating scent. She got closer to the woman and took in another large breath, pulling her scent deep into her lungs. The Wonderland guest attempted to pull away, again stopping when the metal pressed into her tender flesh suit.

The barbed wire was wrapped neatly around her frame, winding its way up her long legs and circling around her bare torso. Her head was encased by metal shards protruding from the wire. Behind her were random strings of colorful blinking lights that hung from the ceiling. She looked like a Christmas present; one that Kyle wrapped her myself.

Just this one time, she thought. *Just this once, I wish this one could be mine forever.* Of course, she knew deep down inside that this could never be. Nothing can last forever.

She shrugged away the thoughts as she inched closer. Their eyes locked and nothing but terror filled the woman's wide, crazed, *perfect* specimens. A burning sensation on Kyle's lower calf pulled her attention away from her guest and she looked down, realizing she'd leaned too close and the barbed wire was poking into her flesh.

"Well shit." She giggled. "Look at that, would ya? I guess that does kind of hurt." Blood formed from those pin-pricks, and smeared up her calf. She wiped it away and gazed longingly at the residue on her fingertips.

The woman attempted to scream, the sound muffled by the bright pink duct tape placed across her lips. Their mixing red trickling blood—the aroma of the woman's insides slowly creeping out onto Kyle's skin grabbed her attention again and she stepped back. She looked greedily upon her guest, then, out of nowhere, feet shuffled on the floorboards above. They creaked and sagged under someone's weight and dust fell from the ceiling.

She glanced up, looking at the wooden slats, squinting to avoid any more dust particles that might fall. A specific shuffle to the walk let her know instantly who it was.

The squeak of the basement door made Kyle look back at her prize and glance toward the stairwell. She found herself more than slightly annoyed by the intruder. *I should have put a DO NOT DISTURB sign on the door before even coming down here.*

Actually, they should know not to interrupt her when she was having her playtime. *It's called respect.* She huffed and let her dissatisfaction be known to her guest of honor. "Damn it," she whispered. "This happens every single time."

It didn't really happen all the time. Kyle was just feeling dramatic and disappointed by being interrupted. Surely anyone would feel the same way.

"It's time for dinner, baby girl." A soft voice drifted down the stairs. Kyle tried her best to keep with the anger that was boiling inside her gut, but her mother's voice calmed her as it always did.

She looked back at the precious, beautiful, mutilated woman before her and clicked her tongue a few times. "I guess we will have to continue this in a few." Kyle bent down and looked directly into her guest's dark brown eyes. "Welcome to my wonderland," she whispered again just to watch her flinch.

She gave the woman another huge smile before standing back up and walking toward the staircase. A dark shadow in the corner of the basement stirred, catching her attention and giving her pause. The figure stayed in the dark, not daring to move into the light, but Kyle knew it was her brother. Lurking. Always lurking. He liked to watch whenever she played with her toys. Normally, he was a good boy and didn't interrupt, so she let him be and left him to enjoy whatever might happen.

"Keep an eye on her for me, Nathaniel." She squinted into the shadows. "Do not... I repeat DO NOT touch her, do you hear me?"

A grunt came from the darkness.

"That's not a yes, Nathaniel. You will be a good boy, won't you?" she questioned him again. She could see the outline of him lean forward and the whites of his eyes appear out of the darkness. He shook his head. His deep, gruff voice came alive when he finally answered. "Me be good."

"Good. Watch her. Don't let her move an inch. Make sure she be good too," she said, echoing his speech patterns. And with that she began to make her way up the stairs. She ignored the woman's squeals as she opened the door and gently shut it behind her.

8

Two

Kyle, or Kyle Lynn to her family, was the first and only daughter to her mother and father—born and raised in a tiny town in the hills of Kentucky—the princess of the family. With three older brothers she would always be taken care of.

Well, she wasn't so much a "princess" as a tomboy. She learned to hunt and fix things around the house. She climbed trees, fished, and played rough with her brothers. Sometimes, she thought *they* saw her as a princess, though. Some men can't see past tits, she guessed.

She sat at the table right next to her mother and served herself a thick cut of bloody steak, probably cut with that weird knife her mama talked to. A spoonful of mashed potatoes splattered on her plate from out of nowhere and she saw her mother place the spoon back into the serving bowl. Kyle sighed and leaned back in her chair, looking defeated.

"Eat up, girl. You need to keep up your strength." Some say she has a twang to her voice, but Kyle didn't hear it.

Kyle's mind wandered for a moment. Settling on a topic that always hit her at unsuspecting times. She became consumed with the thought of how many things in life failed to go as planned for most people. Hell, sometimes even when it did go as planned it didn't turn out exactly how you thought it would. It could never be perfect—for anyone.

That was her life in a nutshell. Always close, but never quite there. Sure, she didn't have to worry about much thus far, but she was only 19 and you never knew when something was going to pop up.

She cut off a large chunk of fatty meat from the steak in front of her and stuffed it into her mouth as she continued to over-think life and its possible challenges. The cow felt like it was melting away to almost nothing on her tongue and finally, she began to chew. The buttery piece squished between her teeth and then slid easily down her throat, coating her esophagus and belly with grease.

"A penny for your thoughts, hun." Her mother finally offered her a smile, her toothless grin making Kyle smile as well.

She gazed at her mother's bright red hair and it reminded her of a blazing fire or the red orange skyline just as the sun was going down on a crisp autumn day. A few silvery streaks formed in the mass of red and her eyes carried a tiredness.

Mother was a looker back in her day. Kyle had seen photos from the '70s, from way before her mother had even met her father. She could have had her pick of anyone and unfortunately, she found herself glued to the bad boys. Or perhaps they were drawn into her bad girl behavior. Either way, it made for an interesting life for their kids.

Kyle's mother, Misty-Dawn Collins was the matriarch of the family. She ran a tight crew with Kyle and her three siblings, especially since their father passed away three years ago. Well, not so much passed away. He died swinging, you could say.

He came home one night, drunk as hell, as was the norm. Kyle couldn't recall a moment when her father wasn't drunk. Anyway, he came at Mom, angry about some such thing—which she probably did do, by the way—and screaming that she would pay for it. Those were his words exactly: "You're going to pay for this one, you stupid cunt."

Kyle was having dinner at the kitchen table and got to see the whole thing. He lunged at her mother, fist barreling toward her face. He didn't count on her being fed up with his bullshit as well and when he took that first swing, she ducked and drove a large kitchen knife right into his chest.

Kyle had kind of figured that would happen someday, so it really didn't surprise her at all. She just looked on while everything went down and continued to eat her stew. She took a large drink of cola as her mother crawled on top of her father, screaming. The knife was beautiful—too beautiful for that house—but Kyle never heard it talk like some of the others. To her, it was just the knife that killed Daddy.

Mom swung down several more times, plunging that ornate blade into his chest. Just like that, it was over for him. And like always, Kyle's brothers gathered together and cleaned up the mess. She'd seen them 'clean up' several situations over the years for Mom and they were very good at it, even when it was their own dad.

Mom looked at Kyle with a twinkle in her eye after the boy's left with Daddy's body. "Remy is happy," she said, but Kyle had no idea who the hell Remy was and thought perhaps her mother had finally lost that final marble.

"Just contemplating life," Kyle said to her as she took another large bite of meat. "It's funny, you know. Just life in general is funny."

"Your life is just starting out, baby girl," her mother responded. "It only gets more confusing as you go along. You'll do well though. Momma taught you well..."

Her words trailed off as she took a bite of her food. Now-a-days she ate more mush than anything because she refused to wear her false teeth. She said they were uncomfortable. It was probably true. Mom would never lie to her. That was a rule of the house. Absolutely no lies allowed.

They were a rowdy crew with the three boys and Kyle, the angel of the family. Again, she was their little princess. Kyle was born several years after her youngest brother, Jacob, so the boys watched over her for their mother. If someone was mean, those boys made sure it would never happen again. She was obviously spoiled.

"Where's the boys tonight?" Kyle asked as she take a spoonful of mashed potatoes into her mouth.

"Nate's around here, somewhere. You know the other two, probably out catching our next meal. Hunting's in their blood." She let out a laugh and pulled her hair back off of her shoulders.

Kyle did know. She knew all too well what they did when they went out. Sometimes, she was lucky enough to join them and when she couldn't they would bring her something to play with, hence her new friend in the basement.

"Mmm," was all Kyle replied as she thought about the first time her brothers took her with them. She had been about 15 and had no clue what their idea of fun was. The black rusty van sped down the road with the four of them. Michael, her oldest brother, was driving and Jacob was riding shotgun. Nathaniel was sitting close to her, as if she needed protection in the back of that van.

Michael had a heavy foot and was pushing the vehicle as fast as it would go. He flew around curves, tossing Nathaniel and her into each other as he went. He would let out a laugh and speed up again prepping for the next curve. Trees flew by as Kyle looked out the window periodically and all she could see was blackness in-between those trees. The roads were narrow and there was nothing but drop-offs on either side.

"It's a long way down," she had said to no one in particular. More laughter echoed throughout the car. Michael turned the lights off and made a sudden turn. It felt like a dirt road and was bumpy. In the darkness Kyle couldn't see shit, but he seemed to know his way.

He slowed down; the car crept slowly up that road and came to a stop when a light appeared in the distance. It illuminated a small home and she could make out the paint peeling around the lighted area. Trees surrounded them on all sides and the boys jumped from the van.

"Now, you have to be really quiet," Jacob whispered as he grabbed something from a duffel bag next to her. He pulled out a partial mask and turned to their middle brother, Nathaniel.

Nathaniel was special, in many ways. He was massive, towering over all of them at 6'5". His huge frame was ripped with muscle and his face slightly disfigured from a little accident he had as a kid. Nathaniel wasn't smart by any means, but he was scary as hell to look at.

Jacob stood on his toes and reached up as he placed the mask on Nathaniel. It covered his mouth and reminded Kyle of a dog's muzzle. He even snarled once it was in place and latched onto to his head. She could only imagine the amount of drool pooling inside of the mask. Kyle knew the wetness would begin leaking out after a few minutes. It would stream down his neck and huge chest before dripping off of him to the ground.

Michael pulled out an ax and handed it to Nathaniel, then grabbed a large knife for himself.

"Ready to play, Nathaniel?" Michael asked him. There was a hushed laughter and the boys moved forward toward the light. "Ready to take out the trash, big boy?"

Nathaniel glared back at her and shook his head yes, as if she were the one speaking to him, then he motioned for her to follow behind.

They must have had this planned for a while, scoping out the place, testing any part of the house that would allow them to enter easily because within what seemed like seconds they were in the dark home. They crept through the little rooms as if they lived here themselves.

Kyle had to admit, she couldn't see shit, and the only thing keeping her from knocking into anything was the boys, who were encircling me. And then we came to a stop and I heard the twisting of a handle. She held her breath, swallowed hard, trying not to let her mind race. Her heart was already doing that. Kyle's anxiety amplified with the twisting and clicking of the handle. The door creaked as it opened.

A night light, plugged into the wall near a window, illuminated the room. She could make out a figure on the bed, wrapped up in old, worn blankets. The cocooned individual didn't move. Jacob silently positioned himself on one side of the bed while Michael made his way to the other. Nathaniel stayed near the foot of the bed.

His hands were trembling a little and he pressed them to his thighs to keep them steady. To keep the other brothers from seeing. Kyle was behind him; he'd never know that she'd seen. He'd never know that her whole body was trembling, not just her hands.

She stared at the boys, having no idea what was going on. Michael motioned for her to come closer. Her feet moved in their direction even though her brain told her to leave. Before she knew it, though, they had the cover pulled back and Jacob and Michael pounced on the person.

Kyle immediately knew who it was. An older boy from school, Darren. Him and his goon friends were a few grades ahead of her and had been torturing Kyle at school for months. It started off with just name calling, spreading rumors throughout school that she was easy and enjoyed 'group' activities. Every once in a while, it would get physical and one of them would hit her. She dealt with it, though, and did her best to ignore everything and just walk away.

Darren and his sidekicks took it way too far a couple of weeks ago. Kyle was on her way home from school and they began following her. Without thinking, she took a shortcut through an alley—she usually did—trying to reach the main road to the bus stop. They grabbed her from behind and pinned her against one of the walls. The brick façade scratched at her back.

"Trying to get us alone, I see." Darren smiled at her and his friends pushed Kyle harder into the wall. They held her arms tightly, giggling with devilish grins.

Darren got closer. "You smell like shit," he whispered. "Don't they allow you to wash up on that farm?"

They boys all laughed.

"Ya, you smell like you rolled around in pig shit," another boy chimed in.

"Your mom likes how I smell." The words just came out of nowhere and she instantly regretted it.

A stinging sensation whipped across her face from Darren's slap. "Don't you ever talk about my mom, bitch."

He pushed himself against her, his hands working their way up her shirt. Grabbing at her special places. "You like that, little pig girl?"

Kyle spat at him and tried to wiggle herself free from the boy's grip. He pushed himself against her again, this time grinding his pelvis against her. "I know you like girls, but that's just cuz ya haven't tasted a real man yet," he said.

"I get first go at her," one of the other boys chimed in.

Darren flashed a menacing look that let him know that wasn't going to happen. "Since you want to be like that, you can go last," he growled.

The boy's grip on her arm loosened when Darren said that and Kyle took advantage of it. Yanking her arms away as quickly as she could, Kyle slipped free and brought her knee up fast. Directly into Darren's groin.

"My dick! *Ngh*... I think she broke my fucking dick!" he screamed, grabbing at his cock and falling to his knees.

A real man, huh? She smirked and then realized she wasn't safe yet.

She took off, running as fast as she could toward the bus stop, hoping they wouldn't chase her. It seemed like it took forever to get there; her lungs hurt and she was close to dry heaving. Coughing and gasping for breath. Lucky for her, a bus pulled up just as she spotted the boys rounding the corner. Darren was taking it more slowly than his friends, walking gingerly with his sore cock. *Serves him right!*

Kyle jumped on the bus, flipping them the bird with glee and not caring if it was the right bus or not. All she knew was that she was at least safe from those boys. As soon as she got off the bus, Kyle ran down the road and up her driveway. All the adrenaline and excitement drained away then, replaced with that familiar heaviness of anxiety and fear.

What if they come for me tomorrow? What will they do then? Why did I have to show off and flip them the bird? Oh fuck, why did I kick him in his tiny dick?

Tears streamed down Kyle's face as she raced to her room and flopped face down onto the bed.

"Hey, little one. Why the rush?" Michael asked as he walked into her bedroom. She sneaked a look at him and saw him leaning against the doorway, hands in his pockets. He was always so casual, and waited patiently for her to collect herself.

She sobbed for a moment, still trying to catch her breath. When she finally calmed, all three of her brothers were in her room, their faces full of sorrow and anguish at her pain. Michael asked again, his patience wearing thin, and Kyle let it all pour out.

"Shit happens," Michael said after carefully listening. "Suck it up; it could have been worse."

"They could have had a poke at ya," Jacob added.

"Well, what if they try to have a poke at me sometime soon?" Kyle asked them, angry that they didn't seem to be taking her seriously. She didn't want to use the 'r' word, but after Darren gyrating his hips against her, she was sure that's where it was headed. Boys didn't get it. "What if they go at me worse next time? What then, huh?"

The boys shrugged and left the room. She spent the days after even more upset with them than the dirty boys who tormented her. How could they let these idiots get away with something like this? They should have had her back, given the boys a proper beating.

She should have known; they did always take care of her in one way or another. However, she had not foreseen them breaking into a house in the middle of the night.

"Is this one of the boys you told us about?" Michael asked.

"Yep." Kyle's voice was a harsh whisper. It was Darren, the ring leader "He tells all his friends bad things about me and then they pick on me. And they make fun of Momma and the farm."

Jacob grabbed Darren by his hair and turned his head to face him. "Sounds like you owe my little sis an apology, big boy." He yanked the boy's head back around to look at me. "Go on then, tell her you're sorry."

Tears were streaming down the kid's face and he yelped when Jacob yanked at his head again. "I said fucking apologize, you little twerp." There was an aggression in his voice Kyle had never heard before.

"I'm sorry, Kyle. I'm so sorry. It won't happen anymore." His voice stuttered as he cried out the words.

A thudding sound down the hallway caught everyone's attention and the room went almost silent, except for the cries coming from the boy on the bed. A figure appeared in the doorway after a few moments—a small man, sporting boxers and a white T-shirt.

"What the hell..."

The words were silenced as Nathaniel brought the ax down on the poor man's skull. Kyle was in shock as blood splattered against the white walls, covering the front of Nathaniel and parts of the floor. He pulled the weapon from the man's head and swung it again, splitting his head in two.

A scream erupted from the other direction and Darren began to jerk around, trying to free himself from her brothers.

"Now, now. We aren't done with you yet," Michael said calmly. "Seems you like to think with more than just that brain in your head. We plan on fixin' that for ya."

He yanked Darren's pants down and in one quick motion made a cut. He tossed the piece of meat and it landed at her feet. Kyle stared blankly at it. It looked like a chicken neck, just smaller.

"What the hell am I supposed to do with that?" she asked him between the screams.

"If you don't want it," Jacob replied, "I can find a few good uses for it." He yanked Darren's head back again and Michael made one last cut across his throat.

That was her first night out with the boys, and one she would never forget. She was scared at first, not knowing what to expect. When Nathaniel plunged that ax into the old man's head, Kyle felt a surge of excitement. Adrenaline consumed her whole body and she wanted more.

She was let in on more family secrets after that. Normally the hunting trips for food came in human form and now that she was grown up enough to share the secrets she was also grown enough to take on some new responsibilities. Preparing the meat for dinners, for example. She was only occasionally allowed to hunt with the boys. Mostly, she would help Mom out with the cleaning and prepping of the meals, though.

The most tender part of the human body was the cheek, she found. The thighs and ass cooked up quite nicely as well. Everyone in the family enjoyed their own thing, and that worked out well. Nathaniel would accept any cut she gave him.

So that's Kyle in a nutshell. She worked hard, played harder, and got lost in her own head a whole lot.

Three

Kyle made up a plate of food for Nathaniel and asked to be excused from the table.

"I have a friend to keep company and I think it's rude to keep people waiting," she said to her mother.

"Have fun, sweetie," Mom said as Kyle stood up and made her way back toward her wonderland. She smiled and appreciated the family support.

As she descended the stairs, she heard the skittering of feet across the floor. Well, more like heavy thudding.

Clomp.

Clomp.

Clomp.

Clomp.

Other than the sound of plodding footsteps, it was eerily quiet. Kyle stopped half way down and turned her head to the side, listening. The heavy clunking of feet across the floor stopped and a deep breathing took over.

"Nathaniel," she called down. "I'm bringing you some food."

She continued down the steps and then stopped dead in her tracks, the plate dropping to the floor. Before her was a bloody massacre. Her breath caught in her throat and she did her best to hold back a scream.

And failed.

"NATHANIEL!"

The single word echoed off the walls as it scraped out of her throat, clawing at her eardrums in the process. Pure rage engulfed her and she saw red, literally.

"What the fuck did you do, stupid?!" The words spewed from her and she flipped on the light, purging the room of any darkness. The whole basement lit up and the little flashing lights seemed dull in the new brightness.

There he was, cowering in the corner and looking pathetic.

"Sorry," he whimpered. "Sorry, Kyle."

"You're sorry?! I told you to fucking leave her alone." Her whole body shook in anger. "She was mine, Nathaniel. She was fucking *mine*, not *yours*!"

"Sorry, Kyle." He sniffled.

"I ought to beat the shit out of you, idiot." Kyle raised her hand like she was going to hit him and he sank further away from her. "You can clean up this mess, and you can eat your dinner off the floor tonight. I'm so done with you."

The big lug pulled his knees to his chest and began rocking back and forth. His whole body was slick with blood; the blood that should have been hers. He began to wipe at his face, and whimper. Even in her rage, the sight of a huge beast crying in a corner made Kyle feel somewhat bad. Not bad enough to let him off the hook, but there was a small soft spot in there somewhere.

Kyle knew her brother had control issues. She knew before leaving the basement that he was there and probably couldn't resist himself. She just thought warning him might do the trick. Keep him from acting on his natural urges. She was wrong.

Kneeling before the horror in front of her, Kyle's knees slid on the blood-covered floor. She sighed heavily and shook her head. *Stupid lug. Stupid, stupid, stupid. Why was I stupid enough to leave him down here with her?*

The woman's body lay in pieces in front of her—arms and legs detached from the torso, head sitting atop the shelf that was home to many of Kyle's books. Blood slowly dripped from the top of that wooden shelf onto the floor and a slow aggravating rhythm.

A wave of dizziness made her head spin and she closed her eyes, trying to will it away. Once again, so close to perfect, and something—or someone—had to come along and ruin it for her.

"I'm going to bed, Nathaniel. This better be cleaned spotless by morning, or else." She pointed her finger at him and glared. "Do you hear me? Spotless!"

"I'm sorry, Kyle," he repeated. A sob escaped from the big guy's mouth and Kyle turned away.

Making her way back up the stairs, she headed to her room when the front door swung open. Michael and Jacob came staggering in, their laughter almost song like.

"Who shit in your Cheerios?" Michael blurted out as he looked at her.

Kyle squinted her eyes at him and growled. She was not in the mood for either of them. Michael's hands went up in defense. "Hey, I didn't do it, whatever it is," he barked.

"Your stupid brother ruined my evening, asshole. I can't stand any of you at times, honestly."

"Whoa, what happened?" Jacob asked. "Your little girlie get the best of you?"

"No, dipshit," she spit back. "I came up for dinner and Nathaniel axed her while I was gone. Now all of you can fuck off and I'm going to bed."

They both began laughing at her, making her anger sky rocket.

"Boys, leave her alone," Mom interrupted. "Go help your brother clean up."

"But we didn't do it," Jacob tried to protest, stopping quickly when Mom held up a finger.

"I said what I said and you will do it."

That's all it took with Momma. The boys, heads hanging low, sighed as they moved off toward the basement.

"And you, little girl. I'm sorry you're disappointed. I understand. However, you will be nice to your brother because you know he can't help himself at times, understand me?"

"Yes, Momma." Kyle turned and slowly took herself to her bedroom—her other sanctuary away from the real world. It was nowhere near as special as her wonderland in the basement, but most of the time she was left alone when she was in her room.

She spent the rest of the night pouting and feeling sorry for herself before sleep finally claimed her and brought some relief from the fiery rage burning inside.

FOUR

"Hey there, sunshine. Feeling any better?" Michael was sitting on the edge of Kyle's bed; the smile on his face was huge. "I know you're upset about that thing with Nate last night, but I have a job for you."

"Fuck off." Kyle rolled over, turning away from him, and pulling the covers over her head.

"I think you may enjoy it, though," he snickered, nudging her in the ribs. "Come on, get up and let me show you."

"I'm not in the mood, asshole. Just leave me alone."

"I can't do that," he replied. "Hey, you know I always have your back. This may not be as exciting as your thing last night, but it's close."

Kyle let out a deep sigh. Just for once in her life, she'd have liked things to go her way. He nudged her again and she pushed the covers down and forced herself to sit up. It took a minute for her to gather herself and before she knew it she was dressed and following her brother out the front door.

The air was humid outside and Kyle could already feel the heat of the day sinking into her skin. Across the yard and into the barn they went. Michael moved fast, his hand gripping hers as he dragged her toward the back of the old, rugged building.

"Go ahead, open the door," he said, his voice laced with excitement. "Go on."

She looked at the metal door for a moment, hoping he hadn't dragged her out there for nothing. Kyle's hand reached out, grasping the handle, and she yanked on it. The door came to life and slowly swung open. A gust of frigid air hit her and refreshed her body. Michael pushed her into the cold storage, flipping on the light as they entered. It buzzed and blinked a few times before fully covering the room with a blinding white glow.

In the middle of the room, on the glimmering metal table, was the body of a woman. Her black hair flowed around her shoulders. Her eyes were closed and she appeared to be at peace. Her skin was tinged with blue, her lips a darker purple. Kyle gasped and approached the table.

The woman's naked flesh drew her in. Perfect breasts and never-ending curves ignited something deep inside of Kyle. Her body shivered as her eyes took her in this new guest.

"She's absolutely stunning, Michael." Kyle's voice was almost a whisper, like she was afraid to disturb the woman.

"I knew you would like her," he said. "Tell me I'm your favorite brother and I have good taste." He let out a devilish laugh.

"What's her name? Where did you get her from?"

"You always have too many questions, girl. Can't you just say thank you and move on with things?"

"I'm sorry. I like to know who I'm working with." She looked at him with annoyance. "Give me a name and tell me what you need me to do."

His smile grew, making him look like the joker from the deck of cards they sometimes played with. "She looks tasty," he said. "Can you prep her for this evening? I think we should celebrate."

"What are we celebrating?" Kyle asked, her eyes still glued to the woman before her.

"Family," he replied. "We are celebrating family." He bounced on his toes and seemed happy about the idea of a celebration. "Plus, we may have a special guest coming over."

All of the rage and hate Kyle felt the night before began to disappear. The idea of a little party definitely made her feel better. And having a specimen so breathtaking before her didn't hurt either.

"She's all yours," Michael said. "Just make sure she's ready in time for dinner."

Kyle's finger traced the curve of the woman's hips and she smile up at her brother. "What time would you like the party to start? That way I can make sure everything is prepped."

His laughter was loud. "Dinner should be ready at seven. I have a few things to do, so that will be a good time."

She nodded. "You got it."

Michael made his way to the door and then turned back. "By the way, her name's Rachel. She was trying to thumb a ride when I found her." Again, laughter, and then he was gone.

Kyle gathered her thoughts and made sure the heavy door was locked before she rolled a small metal tray over to the slab where the woman was waiting. She checked out the tools displayed on the little platter. There were so many sharp objects to choose from and only a small amount of time to accomplish everything that needed to be done.

She made a note in her head of what she needed to do while she slid out of her clothes, not wanting to ruin a new pair of jeans. She crawled up onto the table, straddling the woman. Her eyes greedily looked down on her prize. She was perfection and her cold flesh felt amazing against Kyle's skin. Reaching over, she picked up a blade and gave her a wink.

"Did you just say something, Rachel?" Kyle put her ear closer to the woman's purple lips and listened. "Oh, you're right, I grabbed the wrong tool. A fifteen blade will not do, I definitely need a number twenty. Good eye."

Kyle placed the scalpel back down on the tray and picked up the larger blade. As she went to make the cut, her hips ground against her and she felt a sensation begin to take control of her groin. She closed her eyes and breathed. Slow. Steady. Breaths.

"Sorry about that, Rachel. Sometimes, well I'm sure you understand. Some things we just don't have control over."

Again, Kyle placed the blade against her flesh and finally made the cut from her neck down. She pulled open the flaps of skin and gazed down longingly at the bone, muscle, and organs inside.

A wetness gathered close to her pubic area and Kyle realized it was her causing it. The dead woman's imagined breaths grew heavy as Kyle began to grind herself against her even more. Kyle's trembling hands fell inside her victim's freshly opened cavity and they squeezed at anything and everything they could. She wrapped her fingers around the sticky, glazed stomach and squeezed, her thighs squeezing in rhythm. Her other hand reached past her lungs, deeper inside. Deep, deep, all the way to the heart she imagined thrumming for her with love and passion. It was fleshy and supple and as she held it her hips moved faster, grinding. The dead beauty's cold flesh was heating up with the friction.

Before Kyle could even attempt to stop herself, she explode with pleasure. Her whimpers filled the empty room and her body shook uncontrollably. She let herself collapse forward against her brother's gift to her and she closed her eyes, her fingers twirling little clumps of her silky black hair.

It took Kyle awhile to gather herself because this was something new to her. She'd been intimate with some girls before, but they were alive. They all had a pulse. It was never like this. Ice box sex on a scorching hot day could just be her favorite thing.

She sat up, and ran her trembling fingers down her torso. Lines formed in the red that was covering her body.

"Looks like we both got lucky today, Rachel." Kyle gave her a smile and then began removing the goods from inside of her. Half of the organs would be fed to the pigs. They loved that shit. She set the liver aside for Jacob and the heart for Nathaniel.

Kyle pulled the butcher knife from the second shelf on the portable tray and worked it through those tender parts of her flesh that made for good grilling. Then she took the flanks and thighs. She separated the different parts and placed them in baggies for later use, keeping out only what they would be using for dinner this evening.

When everything was separated, she opened the door, her ice-cold flesh melting in the heat.

She took her time walking back to the house, letting herself thaw out.

"Get in this damn house, girl." Mom's voice brought her out of her pondering. "You have no sense at all, do you?"

"What did I do?" Kyle went over things in her head and couldn't figure out why her mother was so upset.

"Just look at yourself," she half shouted. "You're covered in filth and you're stark naked! Someone could have pulled up and seen you. And then what?"

"No one ever comes out here, Momma. And I didn't want to ruin my clothes—"

"Go take care of yourself right now." She cut Kyle off before she could respond. "Now, do you hear me?"

"Yes, Momma." She hung her head and walked past her. "Tell Michael everything is ready. He just has to put it all away. It's all separated for him."

Kyle quickened her pace up the stairs and jumped into the shower, letting the water wash away the afternoon's mess. She watched as the water rolling off of her went from dark red to pink and then clear.

FIVE

"Today we celebrate each other," Michael said, hand in the air with a glass full of beer. "A family that does for one another and keeps their shit together. I love you all."

They were all gathered around the dining room table, which was covered with a meal that looked incredible, if Kyle said so, herself. Several choice cuts of meat sat in the center of the long wooden table with delicious sides surrounding them. Michael really put some time into this little celebration, and she was impressed with her big brother.

"And we have a special guest," he continued. A huge smile spread across his face, and slow footsteps approached from behind. He stepped aside, and an old woman steadied herself with a cane. Her paper-thin wrinkled skin sagged away from her bones.

Her frame shook, and Kyle's eyes focused on her balding head, patches of gray hair here and there. Her eyes were sunken, and dark circles and bags had formed long ago. Michael placed his hands on the woman to steady her.

"Momma, what are you doing here?" Kyle's mother's voice broke the brief silence that hung in the air. "I mean, when did they let you out?"

Grandma shuffled slightly, and Michael pulled out a chair for her to sit. Kyle swore she could hear the woman's bones creak as her knees bent and her body plopped down. It made her skin crawl as she looked at her. In all her years of life, she had never laid eyes on this woman. She was deemed insane and placed in a mental institution months before Kyle was born. All she'd ever heard were stories, mostly from people around town, about the evil woman who lost her mind and did wretched things to her family and others.

Some rumors were about a love affair with the sheriff in town. When he didn't leave his wife for Granny, she kind of lost it, and to keep things peaceful, he created an elaborate story to get her locked away. Who really knew the truth, though, other than Grandma and the Sheriff?

Kyle would turn her ear to listen to the chatter, trying to piece together the hows and whys of her grandma being locked away. All gossip would stop, though, when they would notice her listening in. She never got much more, and Mom never talked about it.

Mom sat next to the ancient woman and gently took her hands into her own. Her fingers gingerly caressed the wrinkles of the woman's hands. Tears formed in her eyes, and she seemed like she was at a loss for words. "I can't believe you're here. I've missed you more than words can say."

"You never visited me, dear." Grandma's voice crackled the way old leather straps did when you bent them against their will.

"They wouldn't let me, Momma. I tried so many times, and they refused to let me in. They said you weren't allowed visitors," she whispered. "Court ordered."

The old woman shook her head in acknowledgement.

"Well, now that we are all here," Michael cut in, "let's eat. I'm starved and we don't want this beautiful dinner to get cold."

He sat down and pulled Kyle down next to him. His hands worked quickly as he began fixing himself a plate full of food, piling it high with meat and sides.

"This looks wonderful," the old woman said. "I'm glad to be home."

The room was silent as they ate, except for the occasional sniffle from Mom. She wiped at her eyes between bites, stealing glances at the old woman beside her. Kyle's eyes stay glued to them, her plate of food being ignored in those intense moments.

"Not hungry?" Michael whispered to her. "You haven't really touched your food. It's delicious."

"I'm sorry. I'm just not feeling myself."

Again, silence enveloped her.

"Well, why don't you help Grandma to her room? I'm sure she's tired from the excitement of coming home." He landed an elbow into her side and gave her a wink. "She will be sharing your room for now until we can get something fixed up for you somewhere else. How's the attic sound?"

"Eh, I'll just put a bed in the basement. Fewer spiders and heat down there." Kyle stood and took Grandma by the hand, helping her to her feet, and then handed her the cane. "Come, Grandma," she said. "Let me take you to your room."

The aging matriarch swatted Kyle's hands away and shuffled forward without me. She heard Michael laugh and shot him a look. This was going to be interesting with a new person in the house, someone who was a complete stranger to her.

"I would like to bathe before bed." Her shaky voice was low, and Kyle could hardly hear her.

"I can help you, Momma." Mom stood and rushed to the other woman's side. "The bathroom is right down—"

"I know where the bathroom is." Grandma cut her off. "Remember, I did live here at some point." She sized Kyle up with a distasteful frown. "The young one can help me. You have cleaning to do; this house is disgusting."

Mom's head drooped as disappointment spread across her face. *Poor Momma. I can see so much love coming from her for her own mother, and she's being told she is a disappointment,* Kyle thought.

I feel for her. And I feel for me; in no way do I want to bathe this old woman.

She reached the bathroom door and turned to me. "Come, girl. Fetch me a robe and then help me out of these clothes. I need a deep cleaning."

Shivers covered me like gooseflesh, and I took a deep breath, throwing my brothers a quick glance. They all smirked, and I wanted to smash them in their ugly heads with a bat.

Kyle made her way toward the washroom and plugged the drain, beginning to fill the bathtub with semi-hot water. After grabbing her a robe, Kyle began to help peel off her clothing. Her skin was paper-thin and sagged in most areas. Her breasts drooped close to her belly button, and a few grey pubes poked out below. A lump formed in Kyle's throat as she viewed her blotchy white flesh.

Taking her hand, Kyle helped her grandmother balance as she stepped over the side of the tub, the water gently splashing as it took in her body. She let out a long sigh. Her flesh swayed with her movements, and Kyle was mesmerized by the flapping. By how her sagging breasts came to a triangular point at the nipple. By how the skin under her biceps seemed to float independently of her arms as she sank further into the warmth of the tub.

"This is nice. They only gave us cold showers at the hospital," she said. She rested back and let the water move around her as she passed her hands through it.

Kyle took a seat on the toilet and picked up a magazine, trying to avoid looking at her grandmother. Thoughts passed through her head about not wanting to get so old that her skin drooped and hung, every part of her thinning and becoming covered in those splotchy, brown age marks.

"Come help me, girl."

"My name's Kyle," she told her, holding back an eye roll. *If she calls me 'girl' one more time...*

"Kyle, that's a good name. Now come wash Grandma's back." She looked at Kyle, her eyes filled with repressed rage. "Come now. I don't bite. Not anymore. They pulled out my teeth."

Kyle almost wanted to laugh, but held it in. She took a rag and soaped it up, lathering up her skin. She closed her eyes and began to hum. "Such a good girl. Get all of me," she said.

Kyle did my best, washing under the skin flaps that hung from her arms and sides. Under those dangling mounds of flesh that were floating on top of the water.

"There you go, Grandma. All done." Kyle rang out the rag and placed it on the side of the tub. "Let's get you out and into bed for the night."

"We're not done, girl." The old lady quipped. "I may be old, but I'm not dead yet. Put some soap on those fingers of yours and stick them inside me. Lord knows, these cobwebs need cleaned out."

Kyle had to keep herself from gagging at her grandmother's words. Her voice remained shaky, yet became very stern. Almost angry. Kyle tried to gulp back the lump that was stuck in her throat.

"Gotta clean the inside too. Do you hear me?"

Kyle's hands began to shake, and she wanted to excuse herself from the room. She'd enjoyed an older woman here and there, but no one her grandmother's age and surely not a family member, other than that cousin she used to make out with back in the day. This was a whole new level of...

Before she could even finish the thought, the old woman had her hand in Kyle's hair, yanking her closer. Kyle let out a shriek as Grandma pulled her face to her own.

"Listen here, *girl*. We do what Grandma says when she says to do it. Do you hear me?"

"Yes, Ma'am." She gasped.

"Good girl. Now get to it."

Kyle took in a deep breath and soaked her hands in soap. As she reached down, her whole body trembled uncontrollably, and she could have sworn she could hear that old woman cackling. She leaned back in the tub, spread her wrinkled legs wide, allowing for easier access, and cringed as my fingers dove into her.

Six

"They have to pay for what they've done," Grandma mumbled over and over between sips of coffee. "We can't let them get away with what they've done to me."

"Who has to pay, Grandma?" Kyle asked.

"All of them. The whole damn town." She tapped her withered fingers on the table. "No one did a thing to help. They can all go to hell."

Well, that will take some work. The thought ran through Kyle's mind as she tried to figure out how they were supposed to take out a whole fucking town of people. Granted, they lived in a small community. All hill people and farms. It would still take some work.

"So, do you have something in mind? Or are you still working this out?"

"Hush, girl." There was an anger in the old woman's voice, and she swatted at Kyle, landing a decent smack across her cheek. Thwap!

"What the fuck, hag?!" The words spewed from her granddaughter's mouth before she could even think about what she was saying or who she was saying them to.

"WHAT DID YOU SAY?!" Her mother's voice shouted from across the room as she stood and headed toward her. "You do not talk to your grandmother that way. Do you want to go to the time-out room?"

Kyle ducked down and shook her head. "I'm sorry, Momma. She caught me off guard. I'm sorry."

"You watch your mouth or you will end up in the bad room, do you hear me?"

"Yes, ma'am."

"We will start with the sheriff. Is he still around?" Grandma clapped her hands together, and excitement took over her face. She looked at everyone, waiting for someone to answer.

"Well, Momma..." My mother paused briefly before continuing. "The sheriff is retired and living in a home for the elderly now. His daughter is currently the sheriff."

"Sheriff Fields?" Kyle asked. "I'd love to play with her."

"It's settled then," Grandma said with a wry smile. "Don't let me down, girl."

"Kyle. My name's Kyle."

"Never mind that. Just take care of the woman and her family." She raised herself from the chair. "I'm going to my room to rest. Won't you help me to my bed, Michael?"

He gave Kyle a smile and a wink as he approached Grandma and took her hand, leading her down the hallway and away.

Kyle excused herself and headed down to the basement, turning on the strings of colorful lights to take away some of the darkness. She'd spent some of the morning setting up her new space, pulling some old pallets together, and placing a mattress on top for a new bed. She added a few rugs and a shelf for her reading materials, and it was already feeling like home—a place she could sleep and play, a true wonderland.

A steady banging on the floorboards brought her out of her thoughts, and she glanced up. The knocking sound sped up for a moment and became erratic, and then she heard Michael let out a low moan.

I hope he breaks her hips. The thought popped into her mind and made her giggle.

She closed her eyes and began planning her next adventure. This time with Sheriff Fields. Erica Fields's short hair was always hidden under her hat. Even when she was not working, she always wore a hat of some sort. Normally, a ball cap. Her dark brown eyes made Kyle's soul shudder. There was a deadness to them. Dull and lurking.

Kyle had always had the hots for her, especially when she was in uniform. Now, she'd get a chance to really give her a try. Her mind wandered and began putting together all the things she wanted to do with her; the vivid images in her mind turned blurry and faded as darkness took her off to sleep.

Seven

"Hi, Ms. Fields," Kyle said as she sat next to the sheriff. She was at the diner counter, waiting for her morning coffee. This seemed to be her routine, even on her days off.

For once the sheriff was not wearing a cap and her hair was sort of spiked. She had on some tight jeans and a plain white T-shirt. Kyle's eyes scrolled the whole package and admired the creature sitting in front on her.

"Well, Kyle. It's been a while since I've seen you in here." She slid the fresh cup of hot liquid closer to herself and tore open two packs of sugar, dumping the contents into her cup.

"I've been busy. You know, taking care of the family and stuff. I'm living the good life, ya know."

"What brings you out today?"

Kyle watched as the sheriff brought the cup to her red lips and took a sip. Steam billowed up around her face. She closed her eyes as she enjoyed that first taste.

"I kind of wanted to see you," Kyle replied. "I was just thinking, perhaps if you're free this evening, I can take you to dinner."

She let out a laugh and gave Kyle a side glance. "Are you trying to ask me on a date?"

Kyle give her a big smile. "And if I was?"

"Sweetie, you are adorable, but you're a bit too young for me."

"A few years, and who's counting anyways?"

She gave another side eye and smiled.

"I can make you growl like the cougar you are," Kyle whispered into her ear and the sheriff's cheeks flushed bright red. "You know, I've always had a thing for girls in uniform."

"Is that so?" She gave the younger girl a look that let her know she'd piqued her interest. Kyle could almost see the thoughts swirling around in her eyes, the possibilities of what could be. "Look, thanks for the invite, but I have to pass. The rumor mill in this town's horrible and if anyone sees us together on a date things could get crazy."

"You could always have me over for dinner, leave the back door open. Let me sneak in." Kyle winked. Her hand inched closer and she ran a finger up the sheriff's arm. Her voice dropped so only she could hear. "Let me show you my wonderland."

The little hairs on the sheriff's arm stood on end and goosebumps spread up and down her. She looked around, perhaps trying to see if anyone was paying attention. The diner was almost empty other than an older couple in a booth at the far end and a single waitress standing near the kitchen door.

"Hmmm." She sighed. "Come over around eight. Take the trail behind my house so no one sees you, please." She raised her cup to her mouth again without taking another look at the girl. "I'll see you then."

Kyle licked her lips and grinned. "You won't regret it, Erica." She stood and walked out of the building. The sun beat down on her as soon as she made it outside and an excitement ran through her whole body.

Her mind raced with ideas, ways to make Sheriff Erica beg for her to stop, mixing pleasure and pain together until darkness consumed her. It was almost a shame that she couldn't keep her. She'd had her eye on Fields for a while and her mind tried to figure out a way to hide the woman away from her grandma.

Nothing would work, though. One of the boys would rat her out; she was sure of it. Kyle shrugged and decided to just enjoy the moments she would have with her new guest.

EIGHT

KYLE'S PALMS WERE SWEATY as she made her way down the narrow path that led to Sheriff Fields's house, making the flashlight in her hands slick with moisture. Adrenaline and excitement made her feet move faster than normal. Her backpack bounced against her as she walked, the contents clanging together.

When she drew close enough to see the light shining from her back porch, she switched off her light and slowed her pace, glancing at her watch. Ten minutes early. *Would Erica mind? Who cares?* Before she knew it, Kyle was standing on her back porch and her hand gently rapped on the metal screen door.

Eyes peeked outside of the blinds and then she was clicking the latch. The handle turned ever so slowly and the door popped open.

"Kyle," Erica said. "I wasn't sure you would really show up."

The young girl winked. "Of course, who would pass up a date with you."

"I don't really have many folks beating down my door. I'm flattered that you seem to think so." She let out a laugh and opened the door more, motioning for Kyle to come inside.

Her visitor placed her backpack on the floor next to the door and followed her into a dimly lit room. A dining table and six chairs sat in the middle of the room. A single candle burned and silverware on placemats adorned the table.

"Have a seat, dinner is almost done." She pulled out a chair, her hand motioning for Kyle to sit.

"We could just get to the good stuff, ya know."

"I spent all day preparing this dinner, we have plenty of time for..." She paused. "Time for *other* stuff, after our meal."

Kyle let out a little huff of air and then sat, watching the sheriff exit the room. She was back a moment later, carrying two steaming plates and handed one off to Kyle before placing her own across the table from the girl. There was a gleam in her eyes that Kyle hadn't noticed before. They sparkled with the light of the candle and Kyle swore she could see desire burning inside.

Taking a small bite of food, Kyle smiled before testing it. It had a nice flavor, but was nothing like Momma's cooking, that was for sure. Or her own. She took a bigger bite and glanced at the fine specimen before her. This would be the night she made her family proud, the night Grandma would get some revenge for what she had been forced to endure, whatever that was.

They ate in silence for half of the meal, Kyle's mind being preoccupied with the things she wanted to do with the sheriff—to her. She caught a smile from her occasionally and was sure to smile back.

"Is everything alright?" Erica asked.

"Wonderful," Kyle said. "You're a great chef." She took another bite of the well-done steak as she smiled through the lie. She could have been nice and left at least a little pink inside.

"Finish up and we can get to the fun stuff." Erica winked.

Kyle moved to raise her fork again and felt her eyes growing heavy. The room blurred and she had to place her hands on the table to balance in the chair, feeling like any second it could tip over. She laughed because she knew she was in trouble and her head is foggy. Waves of sound danced before her eyes and the room spun out of control.

"Well now, that took longer than I thought it would," Erica said. "Normally this stuff knocks a person out within a few minutes."

Kyle wanted to ask her what she had done—what she planned on doing. Nothing but mumbles fell from her lips. A dampness slid from her mouth and down her chin.

Erica's hands were on her, then. "Don't fight it, Kyle. Just let it happen."

In that moment, Kyle wished she had told her family what she was up to. She tried to surprise them and once again things did not go as planned.

Her eyelids twitched and then closed, her body still fighting the darkness and failing.

NINE

Kyle's eyes flew open and everything was still black. Her body ached, pins and needles running up her spine and she gasped for air. It felt like she was suffocating and every inch of her body hurt. It felt like she was dragged down several flights of stairs and each piece of her hit every step on the way down. She blinked several times, trying to find a light source, but blackness was all that surrounded her.

"Are you awake?" a voice asked from the void. "You've been out for quite a while." It was Erica; she was sure of that, but it sounded tinny, like it was coming from a speaker. "You still up for some fun?"

Kyle's skin was freezing and she could feel cold hard metal beneath her. *Could this be how my friends feel when we play? Is the terror I'm feeling right now exactly how they feel when they get to be a guest at my wonderland?* She attempted to move, trying to relive some of the pain that encased her, but her body didn't budge.

A light flickered and slowly showed her surroundings. Grey concrete walls surrounded her and the room appeared to be almost empty. Almost. Sitting on a little wooden table next to Kyle was her backpack, the contents emptied out on the flat surface. The metal on the hand saw shone in the light and the blades of the scalpels gleamed with pride.

"You *are* awake," Erica said excitedly. This time the voice was right beside her—in the room with her. "Welcome back. As you can see, I unpacked your bag for you."

"What the hell do you think you're doing?" Kyle's question hung in the air for several moments as Erica looked at her. "How about you let me go and we forget this happened?"

"How about...no." There was no thought behind her words.

"If anything happens to me..."

"Blah, blah blah." Erica cut her off. "Your family has been a disgrace to this town for way too many years. Your brothers will do nothing. Your mother will do nothing. I'm sure they don't even know you're here, do they?"

"They always know when I leave the house and where I am going."

"Mmhmmm," Erica replied while picking up one of the scalpels from the table. "I've had you for two days and no one has come looking for you, which leads me to believe you are lying." She ran the blade down a section of Kyle's thigh causing the girl to wince in pain. "Why did you bring toys to our party?"

"You know, I always carry stuff with me. You never know when you might need them."

"I see." She ran the blade down another section of Kyle's thigh. "I didn't know you liked to play...rough," she said.

"I'm not going to beg for you to let me go, so if that's what you want, it's not going to happen."

"Oh, I didn't think you would beg for anything. I knew you would be coming for me, though, since your grandma is home."

Kyle's face contorted with her words.

"That's right, I know your grandma was released. They called as soon as she was wheeled out the doors. It's good to have friends on the inside. And well, our families always had issues with each other." She placed the scalpel back on the table and gave me a wink.

"I don't know what you're talking about. I don't know about any issues between anyone," Kyle lied as she struggled to loosen the straps holding her down.

"Stop lying to me, little girl!" Erica yelled as she slammed her hands on the table that was holding Kyle hostage. "Your family is *shit*. Do you think I don't know what you guys do? Do you think the town doesn't know how *sick* you guys really are? Everyone knows to stay away from the Collins family."

"So then, you plan to take us all out or something?"

"I'm going to have fun with you. Isn't that what you want-ed?" She ran her hand over the girl's bare flesh, fingers circle around her left nipple.

"I'm not much of a bottom, perhaps you can let me go and..."

"That's not going to happen." Erica picked up the saw and ran her finger along the jagged teeth, the desire in her eyes making Kyle uncomfortable. "This will require some work, but let's see how much I can make you squirm," she whispered as she placed the cold metal to Kyle's shoulder.

A movement caught Kyle's attention then, something behind Erica approached with muted footsteps. The dark figure creeping up on them went unnoticed by her captor and she felt the teeth of the saw bite into her flesh. Kyle screamed, guttural and raw, and she felt weirdly turned on, but it was cut short.

There was a popping sound, like someone taking a sledge hammer to a melon. Erica's head exploded, covering her with a warm red wetness. She could see Nathaniel standing over her as Erica's body slumped to the floor.

"Fucking took you long enough," Kyle spat.

"Next time tell us where you're going and it won't be a prob-lem," Jacob said as he stepped out from behind Nathaniel. His hands worked quickly as he undid the straps holding Kyle down. "This is going to need some stiches." He pressed his fingers into the ragged cut on her shoulder and Kyle swung her other hand at him, landing a good smack to his chest. "Momma will fix you up when we get you home."

Kyle tried to sit up and the room spun around her. Nathaniel didn't miss a beat and grabbed hold of her, slinging her over his shoulder. He carried his sister toward the door, towards freedom.

Ten

"Hey there, Devyn." Kyle's words were a whisper as she took a picture of the person before her. Devyn's arms were spread out, hands held in place by two thick rusty spikes. They looked majestic hanging before her, like Jesus displayed on the cross.

Her heart raced in excitement. This had been a long time coming; while her wounds from Erica healed, Kyle had gone over every little detail, made notes, and calculated every move to ensure she wouldn't become the victim again.

Devyn mumbled something she couldn't understand. Everything was garbled.

"Cat got your tongue?" she asked. She dug into her pocket and found the moist morsel, pulling it out. "Oh wait, here it is." She giggled.

Kyle snapped another photo before putting her camera down. She got closer to Devyn, so close that she was sure the heat of her breath was flowing down their neck.

"I had a run in with your mother a few weeks ago. It was pretty nasty. She tried to remove my arm." Kyle pulled up the sleeve of her shirt, showing the fresh scar. "If it wasn't for my brothers, I'm sure she would have removed it without a second thought."

More jumbled words and something that sounds like a scream escaped Devyn. Tears ran down their face and she felt pleased with their reaction.

"Her bad luck, I guess. She lost her head. That doesn't mean *we* can't have some fun though." She gave Devyn a poke to the side. "Do you want to play with me, Devyn?"

She wriggled, trying to get away. It was useless and she knew it. Kyle got even closer, her body leaning into her guest's. She brought her lips to Devyn's ear and ran her tongue along the lobe.

"Welcome to my wonderland," Kyle whispered.

THE PAST NEVER DIES

ROWLAND BERCY JR.

Eleven

"What the fuck was that?" Kyle exclaimed, glancing around in shock as something fell with a loud crash behind her. She yanked the knife out of Devyn's side, the wet tearing sound prompting a stifled cry of pain from her captive. "I'll be right back. Don't you go anywhere," she taunted, setting the bloodied knife on the table beside him.

She paid no attention to Devyn's sobbing as she started searching the basement for the source of the disturbance.

Turning around, she noticed that a bucket filled with rusty, blood-stained knives—mementos from some of her previous adventures—had toppled from its spot on a shelf. This confused Kyle since the pail had been securely placed on the shelf before it fell.

"How the hell?" she muttered as she bent down and started to gather the blades and place them back in the bucket. She paused and smiled when she picked up a 9-inch kitchen knife, the one she had used on Rachel; a gift from Michael.

Kyle placed the restocked bucket back on the shelf and grinned mischievously as she made her way back to Devyn, ready to complete her task. Dinner time was approaching, and Momma needed some fresh meat for her recipe: Roast Rump with Garlic and Herb Stew.

On her way back, Kyle walked through a frigid patch that sent a shiver down her spine and made her teeth chatter. Then, as quickly as it came, the cold vanished with her next step.

Hugging herself to shake off the chill, Kyle's focus returned to the present when Devyn started whimpering again.

"Hold your horses. I'm comin'." Kyle teased, temporarily forgetting about the spilled bucket of knives to focus on the task in front of her.

Twelve

Misty Dawn Collins shouted up the stairs, "Jacob, get your butt down here now, it's time for church!" Despite the family's rather unconventional habits, Misty had to put on the facade of a dutiful daughter now that Grandma, a hypocritically devout woman who thought that 'Thou Shall Not Kill' was more a suggestion than commandment, was back home. Not wanting to endure it by herself, she decided Jacob would join them for the Sunday morning service.

"Momma, I don't want to go," Jacob complained as he reached the bottom of the stairs, only to receive a backhand to the mouth from Grandma Matty May Collins, who was standing beside Misty.

"Don't you sass your momma, boy."

Jacob rubbed his stinging cheek as he glared at his grandmother, then muttered under his breath, "Sorry, Mom."

Misty shot him a warning look to behave, lest he receive more than a smack and harsh words from his grandmother. "Now help your grandma to the car."

"Yes ma'am," Jacob replied as he took hold of his grandmother's arm and led her away a little too roughly. He felt a small bit of satisfaction from the rebellious act of wearing his HAIL SATAN T-shirt beneath his oversized shirt during service.

"Where are the others?" Matty asked over her shoulder, stumbling as Jacob pulled her along.

"Oh, th-their busy this morning." Misty stuttered in response as she made to follow Matty and Jacob to the car. She took one step and let out a startled cry as someone placed a hand against her back and shoved her so hard that she went tumbling to the ground.

Misty let out a sharp cry as the unforgiving hardwood floor slammed into her with brutal force. Her jaws clenched against the searing discomfort surging through her wrist like a wildfire. The fall had contorted it in a grotesque, unnatural twist, unleashing a torrent of red-hot agony that shot up her arm like a bolt of lightning. She grit her teeth with fierce determination, cradling her throbbing wrist against her body as if trying to shield it from further torment.

When Jacob heard his mom fall, he snapped around and hurried to her side. "Mom, are you okay? What happened?"

Misty glanced back, expecting to see Nathaniel or one of the other kids behind her, but saw no one. Her forehead wrinkled in confusion.

"It felt like someone pushed me," Misty murmured as she let Jacob assist her to her feet.

"But nobody else is here," Jacob replied. "You must have tripped."

Before they could ponder the situation any further, Matty, leaning against the doorframe, burst into laughter. "Girl, you're about as clumsy as they come. Always tripping over your own two feet. Shake it off, and let's get to church before the service starts."

With another confused glance over her shoulder, Misty decided to attribute her fall to her own clumsiness and did as her mother ordered.

Thirteen

The Collins family sat gathered around the kitchen table, with Jacob still muttering about shitty church and how nobody appreciated his shirt. It'd been quite some time since Misty had prepared Rump Roast Stew, so everyone had eagerly been looking forward to dinnertime.

The hint of Devyn's boiling flesh wafted through the air as Misty staggered into the dining room, balancing a towering pot that belched with clouds of steam. Everyone perked up, mouths watering in anticipation.

As she set down the heavy iron pot on the table with an thud, her family let out appreciative grunts and groans—all except Grandma Matty who remained silent but for an occasional rattle from deep within her chest.

Nathaniel eagerly stood and reached for the soup ladle resting in the pot. Ready to scoop a helping of the pale and mottled meat, which had been expertly cut into large, chunky pieces. The juicy, fatty deposits of human flesh floated in the bubbling broth, coating the surrounding carrots and potatoes in an oily sheen.

It looked utterly delectable.

Before he could seize hold of the serving spoon, Grandma Matty snatched her wooden cane and rapped him across the knuckles.

"Mind ya' manners, boy!" She spat before shooting him a look cold enough to stop him in his tracks and force him back into his seat. She chuckled menacingly before taking up the ladle and serving herself first, gleefully plunging it into Devyn's soupy remains.

The rest watched on hungrily as she chewed, mouth open, her eyes rolling back in ecstasy with each bite; juicy morsels disappearing whole down her false-toothed throat. After Grandma had gotten her fair share, Nathaniel picked up his own bowl eagerly, yet carefully avoiding eye contact lest he be admonished for sloppiness again. Everyone followed suit...

Matty had been back from her time in the mental institution for just over two weeks. Although Frank Collins, Misty's late husband, had been mentioned briefly, Matty remained unaware that Misty had killed Frank. He was currently—and forever would be—laid bricked into the basement wall. It hadn't ended well for him after he'd come home drunk one too many times and attempted to assault Misty, who had defended herself by plunging a large kitchen knife into his chest.

"Where's that good for nothin' husband of yours, girl?" Matty asked, glancing up at her daughter from under bushy eyebrows.

Misty swallowed hard before she replied, "Oh, he, uh... He's away hunting." She tried to act nonchalant, as if it were nothing more than an everyday occurrence. Which in reality it wasn't, as Frank, when he was alive to do so, and the kids often crossed state lines to capture their prey, avoiding hunting near home to prevent drawing unwanted attention.

As soon as Misty had uttered her last words, the temperature in the dining room plummeted as an icy current whipped through the air. Silverware and fine china clattered noisily on the table, catching the stunned attention of the unsuspecting family. The distant clamor of cabinets flying open and crashing closed from the kitchen added to the chaos.

Full plates of Devyn stew flew into the air, propelled by invisible forces, smashing against the walls and splattering their contents across horrified faces. Shrieking in terror, the family members scrambled away from the table, trying desperately to evade flying tableware.

As swiftly as it had begun, however, the commotion ceased, and an eerie hush descended upon them as the ghostly figure of Frank Collins materialized, hovering above the dining room table. His emaciated features contorted into a grimace of pure rage and vengeance as a translucent hand shot out towards the chandelier, sending it swinging wildly. His icy eyes narrowed as he glared at Misty.

"That's quite the tale ya' spinnin', girl," Frank said with a growl that sent shivers down everyone's spine—except for Grandma Matty, who simply shook her head and scoffed dismissively while reaching for another piece of meat from the pot in front of her.

Fourteen

"For fuck's sake, Misty!" Frank's ghostly voice boomed through the room. "You couldn't even bother to come up with a better lie? Huntin'? Really?" He threw his ghostly hands in the air.

Grandma Matty rolled her eyes and continued chewing on her human meat thoughtfully before wiping her mouth on her sleeve. "Well, as I live and breathe, I guess Misty finally got tired of all your bullshit, huh, Frankie boy," she said, using the pet name she knew he hated. "I knew it was only a matter of time until one of you killed the other." She cackled deviously, her laughter bouncing off the walls.

Jacob, Michael, and Kyle cowered under the table, their wide eyes darting between their ghostly father, Misty, and seemingly unfazed grandmother. Even in death, Frank's presence was enough to strike fear into their hearts. Except Nathaniel, who despite his imposing size, had always been a mamma's boy and despised the way Frank treated Misty.

Grandma Matty, too, just seemed more amused than anything else, and continued chomping on Devyn. She slurped down a piece of the girl's butt check, and wiped oil from her mouth with the back of her hand.

"Frank," Misty began, her voice cracking slightly as she attempted to placate her husband's spirit. "I was just—"

Frank cut her off with a menacing glare. "Yeah, I know what you were 'just' doin'. His spectral form floated closer to Misty.

"It was self-defense!" Misty protested. "You were drunk—Again! And you know how you get when you drink!"

"Self-defense my ass," he spat, his translucent form shimmering.

Grandma Matty's laughter filled the room as she tapped her cane on the floor, enjoying the tense situation between her daughter and son-in-law—or son-in-ghost, as it now was. "Frank, Frank, Frank," she cackled, "you should've known better than to mess with my Misty. The girl can be quite resourceful when backed into a corner." She took another leisurely bite of Devyn's chewy ass meat before continuing. "Why, I remember one time when we were on a trip to..."

"Mother!" Misty interrupted. "This is not the time for your storytelling!" she hissed through gritted teeth. Her eyes never left Frank's specter, which was now pacing back and forth across the dining room ceiling like a caged animal.

Ignoring her daughter, Matty continued. "Frank," she said in a patronizing tone. "You're just upset because Misty has moved on without you. Well, surprise, the world keeps spinning." She pointed her cane at her son-in-law's ghostly form. "Now, you can either accept your lot in life...er...death...or whatever, or you can move on to...well, wherever it is you're supposed to go."

Frank's ghostly features darkened, if that were even possible. "Move on?! I'm not going anywhere until this murderous whore takes a one-way trip to Hell with me!" Frank, now hovering cross-legged just above the fireplace mantle, shouted with a ghastly gusto.

He surveyed the scattered tableware on the floor, and with only a thought, a 7-inch steak knife levitated up from the ground. With another thought, Frank rotated the knife and aimed it at Misty.

FIFTEEN

"Frank, don't," Misty whispered, raising her hand defensively as she backed away, her eyes wide with fear at the sight of the gleaming blade.

Frank chuckled, extending his ghostly hand toward Misty.

"You no hurt Mama!" Nathaniel shouted, stepping in front of Misty to protect her.

"And what are you gonna do to stop me, sloth?" Frank laughed, mimicking the line, "Ruth! Ruth! Baby! Ruth!" from *The Goonies*, which made him laugh even more.

"You no laugh at me!" Nathaniel bellowed.

"Fuck it!" Frank said, his voice dripping with disdain. "I never thought the retard was mine anyway. Something like that could've never come from these here balls," he sneered, grabbing a handful of ghostly crotch with a crude laugh before flinging both hands into the air. Instantly, every knife, fork, and sharp utensil in the room shot up, hovering menacingly, all aimed at Nathaniel.

"No!" Misty shrieked in horror as Frank, with a vicious grin, thrust his arms toward the boy. In a deadly blur, the utensils launched towards Nathaniel. He barely had a moment to comprehend the danger before multiple sharp objects stabbed into his body.

Nathaniel's eyes widened in terror as he felt the icy bite of cold steel invading his flesh. One wickedly sharp blade glinted in the low light shot across the room and plunged into his shoulder, sending a shockwave of pain rippling through his body. Another blade followed, embedding itself with a sickening thud just below his ribcage. A heavy fork, its prongs gleaming, pierced his bicep, while a serrated steak knife sank deep into the soft, vulnerable flesh of his upper thigh, the jagged edge tearing through muscle with ease. Crimson blood mixed with clear, viscous ocular fluid trickled down his face in clumpy rivulets as the handle of a knife protruded from within the depths of one of Nathaniel's eye socket. He thrashed, desperately trying to dislodge them but they were lodged too deeply; each twist worsening the agony that coursed through him.

Nathaniel's dying screams filled the room, mixing with the cries of his terrified siblings only to be met with Frank's malevolent cackling and Misty's desperate pleas for help. After expending much of his energy to eliminate Nathaniel, Frank's spectral form began to flicker in and out of focus, as he floated above the chaos he had created.

Grandma Matty looked on, enjoying the macabre display with a twisted grin. "Well, I must say, Frankie boy, that's quite cruel even by your standards. Nevertheless, I'm impressed." She chuckled approvingly.

"If you think that was impressive what till ya see what I have planned for you, you wrinkled ol' bitch." Frank responded with a menacing growl.

"You're a floating lie, and I can see right through you." Matty cackled, grabbing a saucer and launching it at Frank. The dish sailed through him and exploded against the wall.

"Clearly, we can't lay a finger on you, but I'm betting Reverend Tumblin can give you the spiritual boot straight to Hell," Matty replied smugly.

"HA! That queer?" Frank laughed. "That fraud couldn't exorcise a ghost if he had the Pope holding his hand and a choir of angels singing backup." He frowned, looking around in confusion, his form blurring until he was almost invisible, then turned his attention back to Misty.

"It's true I can't attend to you here and now, as I'd like. But just try to stay out of my way! Just try!" Frank said, attempting to imitate the Wicked Witch from the *Wizard of Oz*. "Fuck this hocus pocus bullshit!" His final words which lingered in the air, echo-

ing as his spirit, depleted of ectoplasmic energy—for now—shim-
mered weakly before vanishing.

Sixteen

After tidying up Frank's chaos, and sending the other kids away for the day to mourn Nathaniel's death, Matty and Misty had spent the morning making dinner. Sure, it was sad and all, but meat is meat, and Nathaniel had turned into enough stew for two weeks—at least.

Matty and Misty sat in the kitchen sipping their coffee, awaiting the esteemed reverend's arrival. They'd agreed it was best to confront Frank's spirit on their own. Misty looked like she'd been on a sleepless marathon, still visibly shaken over her son's untimely demise, and the fact that she'd had to chop him into pieces while crying, "My baby, my baby."

"Girly, ain't no use in crying over spilled milk. Nathaniel's back-fat alone is gonna feed the lot of us for weeks to come."

"I know, but he was my baby." Misty pouted.

"He was unpredictable. And, well, not the sharpest tool in the shed," Matty retorted, hobbling over to the stove to flip the sizzling strips of Nathaniel bacon. "We're better off without him. Plus, you've got bigger fish to fry right now. Your ghostly, vengeful husband probably won't rest until he's offed you, and more importantly, maybe *me*. You can mourn the derp later."

Misty sniffed, letting out a long breath. "I suppose you're right." She took another sip of coffee and nodded slowly as if coming to terms with reality bit by bitter bit, like it was an extra-strong brew kicking in. The sound of tires on gravel outside the house caught their attention.

"Come in, Reverend," Matty said, making space for the preacher and his off-sider, Lucas. A handsome Mexican choirboy with a body that could inspire prayer or invoke damnation, his demeanor a blend of serenity and sexiness. The choirboy seemed to be the reverend's constant companion for reasons rumored yet unknown. Lucas's choir robes did their best to hide his corn-fed physique, but to be honest, it was like trying to hide a glitter bomb explosion behind a sheer curtain.

Prior to his arrival Matty and Misty had decided it best not to divulge to the Reverand the gruesome details of Nathaniel's demise.

Afterall, some truths were better left buried – or simmering quietly on the stove.

The reverend entered the room, inhaling the scent of sizzling bacon. "Matty, whatever you're cooking smells divine."

"Why don't you and your assistant sit in the dining room, and I'll fix you all a breakfast plate." Matty guided the men and Misty to the dining area.

"No time for breakfast," the reverend replied. "If what you're saying about Frank is true, we've got to handle him pronto," he added, glancing around anxiously. "Have you seen him since last night?"

"Not since he turned dinner into a poltergeist party," Matty grumbled. "But he's been causing quite the commotion all night. Banging on walls, knocking things over. He's a ghost with a vendetta. If he weren't already six feet under, I swear I'd..."

Reverend Tumblin cleared his throat and glanced reproachfully at Matty.

"Sorry Pastor," Matty responded. "It's been a stressful night."

Reaching the dining room, Misty chimed in, "This is where he made his grand entrance."

Looking around the room which, even after being straightened up was still a wreck. After taking in the scene, Reverend Tumblin cleared his throat. "I've got my Bible and my holy swag. Lucas will lend his assistance. We'll give this exorcism thing a whirl, but I can't promise you a miracle."

Reverend Tumblin placed his hand on Misty's shoulder, "Fear not, my child. We shall cast out this demon. Lucas, come and join me in the exorcis—"

88

Seventeen

Before he could finish, Frank's ghostly apparition materialized and floated above them in the center of the room, a malevolent grin on his ethereal face. Glowing red eyes bored into Matty and Misty. "So...you've brought reinforcements? I'm flattered, or rather, I would be if they stood a ghost of a chance against me!"

The reverend and his choirboy, Lucas, gaped at the figure.

"Good to see you, Reverend," Frank quipped, eyeing the holy man who stood there like he'd just seen a ghost. Which, technically, he had. "It's a bit of a change seeing you from this angle. I remember when I was just a wee lad, I was usually on my knees looking up at you, and let's just say, prayer wasn't exactly on the agenda in the confessional booth."

The reverend slowly regained his composure and turned to face the ghostly apparition, crossing himself. His voice lowered in determination as he spoke again. "Be gone, Master of Lies," he began, peeking over his shoulder as a crimson flush spread across his cheeks. "You'll not harm this family any further," he said with false bravado. "The power of Christ compels you! The power of Christ compels you!"

Frank let out a sinister chuckle at Reverend Tumblin's feeble attempt to exorcise him and then stopped with a look of anguish plastered across his ghostly visage.

"Oh, sweet baby Jesus!" Frank yelled in a shrill falsetto. "NO! You can't do this to me... NO! NO!! NO!!!" he howled, shaking his head from side to side.

Lucas stood by with his head bowed mumbling what might have been prayers, or maybe the lyrics to a love song, while the Reverand delivered the exorcism like a man reading from a warranty manual.

Convinced God was on his side and that he was moments away from sending Frank packing, Reverend Tumblin grinned wide. But his triumphant smile quickly crumbled when Frank suddenly stopped his theatrical antics and erupted into maniacal laughter.

"Bahahahaha! You really thought you could get rid of me that easily? Oh, that's rich! You should see the moronic look on your face. Absolutely priceless."

Feeling humiliated, Reverend Tumblin collected himself and continued with the exorcism. He started reciting random Bible verses from memory. "Here she lusted after her lovers, whose genitals were like those of donkeys and whose emission was like that of horses."

Matty and Misty's eyes widened in disbelief as they processed the shocking words, while Lucas flushed three shades of red from embarrassment, none of them flattering.

"A bible verse about donkey dick, and horse spunk from Sister Tumblin. Hardly a surprise," Frank exclaimed, his voice shaking with uncontrollable laughter. He spun through the air performing barrel rolls, his amusement evident in every twist and turn.

The reverend cleared his throat and adjusted his glasses. His voice wavered as he belted out another verse. "Behold, I will corrupt your seed, and spread dung upon your faces, even the dung of your solemn feasts; and one shall take you away with it."

Frank's laughter erupted once more, echoing off the walls as translucent tears from his amusement traced paths down his spectral face. "Kinky bastard's into scat," he jeered, his voice thick with mockery. "Father, it sounds like you'll need to recite far more than just three Hail Marys to atone for your heathenistic ways."

Reverend Tumblin's face turned a deep crimson, his cheeks burning with embarrassment as he sputtered defensively. "What! That's not what I meant!" His voice was sharp and outraged, as he struggled to regain his composure amidst the teasing.

"Reverend, I could keep this up all day, but I've got placed to go and people to kill so let's get on with it shall we."

"Frank, stop it! Leave us alone!" Misty shouted. "What's done is done. Why don't you go and haunt someone else?"

Frank ignored Misty's pleas and without warning flew into Reverend's Tumblin's body wherein he began to control the man like a puppet on a string.

With clumsy movements, Reverend Tumblin began to dance around the room to an imaginary tune, singing "A Whole New World" from *Aladdin* at the top of his lungs—in perfect falsetto. Lucas stood frozen, unsure of what to do as his mentor shamefully pranced around the room.

Misty covered her face with her hands in embarrassment while Matty doubled over with laughter. "I'm sorry," she said between wheezes of laughter. "I'm sorry...but...this is...too...much!"

Frank danced the reverend out of the dining room and up the stairs. Misty and Lucas did what they could to restrain him, but his unpredictable movements and the fierce flailing of his arms and legs made approaching the possessed man next to impossible.

The reverend pranced and twirled up the stairs like a drunken ballerina, his robes billowing around him as he went. The performance ended abruptly as Frank, still in control of Tumblin's body, halted the good man at the top of the stairs.

Misty, Matty, and Lucas, still reeling from the bizarre scene unfolding before them, could only watch as Frank-possessed Reverend Tumblin looked back over his shoulder and winked at Misty before he began tipping backward.

The reverend let out a piercing, heart-wrenching scream as gravity wrenched his body into a merciless descent down the stairs. Each step down was a cacophony of agony as the air filled with the sickening symphony of bones snapping and crunching against each other as his body resounded down the unforgiving wooden steps. His flesh, unable to withstand the relentless assault, split open, allowing shards of shattered bone to pierce through the skin like grotesque white daggers. The once strong ligaments stretched beyond endurance, ripped and tore with vicious, echoing pops.

As he plummeted down the stairs, his body slammed into the wall and railing with savage force, detonating clouds of plaster into the air. Each bone-jarring collision was accompanied by the violent crash of glass, as picture frames fell from their hooks, their piercing shards littering the cold, unyielding hardwood steps.

In a desperate, primal bid to halt his descent, one flailing hand clawed at the banister. The grip was fleeting, and with a stomach-churning, wet crunch, his wrist snapped like a brittle twig. The reverend's screams tore through the air as his relentless plunge continued. Each punishing impact on the merciless steps shattered his bones with ruthless precision.

When he hit the next step, his leg snapped with a grotesque pop, bending at an impossible angle that scoffed at all-natural law. His body then twisted into a chaotic somersault, and with a horrifying shatter, his right arm was annihilated against the next step. He flipped backward, crashing down on his neck with a spine-chilling crack that silenced his cries in an instant, leaving only the eerie echo of his final scream reverberating in the air.

The group at the bottom of the stairs scattered in frantic terror as the reverend landed heavily at the foot of the staircase with a sickening thud. Blood pooled around him, a gruesome testament to the savagery of his fall, seeping into every crevice, staining the floor in dark shades of crimson.

The group looked up from the crumpled body at the foot of the step up to the top landing to see Frank's ghost hovering in midair, smiling maliciously.

Matty was the first to speak. "Well Frank, that was rude. That was pretty fuckin' rude," she said, poking at Reverend Tumblin's body with the tip of her walking cane. "Don't ya think it's time to stop all this nonsense and move on?"

"I'll move on when your daughter has paid the price for killin' me, and not a second sooner. And if this here don't make it clear as day, anyone who tries to stop me from gettin' my revenge is gonna face the music." The sound of fast approaching sirens drew everyone's attention.

"Oh great, just great, who went and called the pigs?" Matty asked, eyeing Lucas and Misty.

"I did," Lucas admitted. "Figured them cops might be able to lend us a hand," he said, looking a bit sheepish.

"Shows what you know, choirboy. The last thing we need is police stinking up the place." She peeked through the blinds and huffed in annoyance. "Well, this day just keeps getting better and better now, don't it? It's Lester Harrison. Erica Field's old man. The last thing we need 'round here is another ex being tangled up in this mess."

Misty glanced over at her ma. "So, the rumors 'bout you and Officer Harrison are true?"

"Oh hush up, girl. You got bigger fish to fry," Matty replied, looking up the stairs at the ghost of her son-in-law who blew a kiss before vanishing.

She whirled around to face Lucas. "You, get Reverend Tumblin outta sight." Lucas stumbled over to the dearly departed pastor and grabbed him by the legs.

"This way," Misty commanded, leading the boy to her bedroom, where Lucas, with Misty's help, unceremoniously crammed the reverend into the closet.

"What about me?" Lucas bleated like a sheep lost in the pasture.

"Umm... If they ask, tell the cops you're staying with us while the reverend is on a pilgrimage to the holy land," Misty said hurriedly. She knew Lucas had been abandoned by his mother like forgotten luggage and that he was now under the church's wing until he turned 18.

"Can I stay with you for real?" Lucas asked, eyes bright with the promise of mischief. "This place is a riot."

"We'll discuss it later," Misty said, suspecting the boy's eagerness to become a permanent fixture in the Collins household had more to do with his budding relationship with her son Michael. She'd noticed how Michael strategically used his bible to conceal certain 'divine revelations' whenever Lucas sang in the church choir. Misty and Lucas then reunited with Matty in the foyer, where she was sure more chaos would be unfolding.

EIGHTEEN

Matty swung open the door, just in time to catch Officer Harrison making his grand exit from the patrol car. She slumped against the wall like a dramatic actress in a B-movie, fishing out a pack of cigarettes from her robe pocket. Lighting one up, she puffed a smoke cloud into the air.

Meanwhile, Misty, who had noticed the decorative yet alarming puddle of Reverend Tumblin's blood at the foot of the staircase, enlisted Lucas's help to drag a luxurious, red paisley rug from the next room, laying it over the crimson mess.

"Matty, you're out? The docs said you'd be stuck in that loony bin for a while," Officer Harrison said with obvious delight walking up the front steps onto the porch.

"Yeah, well, apparently my stellar manners charmed the parole board," Matty replied with mock indifference, though she'd be lying if she said seeing Lester Harrison III didn't dampen the crotch of her dusty depends.

"Lester, what are you doing here? I thought you had retired. Last I heard you were living in a home," Matty inquired, exhaling a fog of smoke that engulfed his face like a vengeful ghost. Misty and Lucas huddled behind her like a curious pair of nosy neighbors.

Officer Harrison coughed and waved away the smoke cloud. "Oh, well, you see, my wife croaked a few years back, and after Erica's murder and Devyn's disappearance, I figured it was time to dust off the old badge. Truth is that retirement was about as appealing as a root canal."

"So sorry to hear about your wife," Matty said with all the sincerity of a used car salesman. In truth, she couldn't care less. She still had a raging crush on Lester Harrison III, and now that his dearly departed was six feet under, Matty suddenly had high hopes of reviving that old flame. "I heard about what happed to Erica and Devyn. That's horrible. Do police have any leads on who could have been involved with what happened to your daughter and grandson?" She went on, tossing a brief, curious glance at her daughter.

"Not yet. We had a few leads, but they all flopped like a fish out of water. Let's face it, Erica wasn't exactly Miss Congeniality. She had a hit list longer than my..." He looked down. "Well never mind. Could've been any one of a hundred people who wanted to give her a taste of her own medicine. Honestly, if you ask me, Devyn's got 'guilty' written all over him. Erica wasn't exactly getting any mother of the Year awards. She probably pushed him to the edge, and he decided to take a permanent vacation from her nagging. He most likely offed her, hopped on the first Greyhound, and skedaddled out of town. And you know what? Can't say I'd blame him if he did. Anyways, the station got a call from Lucas about some sort of disturbance. I was the closest, so I figured I'd pop by and see what all the hubbub was about." Lester tipped his hat in greeting to the gathered crowd. "Something about an exorcism gone wrong. You know, the usual Tuesday afternoon in this town."

Misty planted a delicate hand on Lucas's shoulder. "Officer, I apologize for the confusion. Turns out it's a classic case of oops, wrong number. Lucas is shacking up with us until Reverend Tumblin gets back from his vacation in the holy land and we decided to have a horror movie marathon last night with *The Conjuring*, and the dear boy here had a nightmare during his siesta. Poor kid woke up thinking the demons were real and not just bad CGI, and dialed 911 in a panic. We've since de-haunted him, so thank you for zooming over like a superhero, but we're all good now."

"Isn't that the reverend's car?" Lester inquired, peering back with a touch of suspicion at the 1992 Cadillac Brougham lounging idly in front of the house

"Uh, yeah. It sure is," Lucas chimed in. "I chauffeured his holiness to the airport yesterday."

"I see. Can I come inside and take a look around?" Officer Harrison asked, glancing over at Matty.

"Sure, why the hell not. Come on in," Matty replied with a sigh, tossing her cigarette to the ground and crushing it underfoot. "Misty, why don't you and Lucas get started on dinner while Lester and I have us a little chat," she added, moving aside to let the officer enter the house.

Stepping inside, Lester surveyed the chaos left in the aftermath of Reverend Tumblin's stairway somersault. "What happened here?" he asked suspiciously.

"Oh, Lester, you know how much of a klutz I am. I tripped and took a spectacular nosedive down the stairs. Thankfully, I didn't break too many bones, but these did take a pop out on the way down," she announced, fishing into her mouth and pulling out her gooey false teeth, still glistening with a generous coating of sticky Fixodent. Matty provocatively ran a slick tongue over her lips and gave her gums a few enthusiastic claps. Lester's eyes widened with forbidden desire. "Why don't you join me in my bedroom? We can, uh, catch up on old times." Matty said with a lop-sided wink of her lazy eye.

"You still have that scandalously tacky policewoman costume I got for Halloween?" Lester whispered, leaning in to ensure no one else heard.

"Why, are you a falsely accused minority in desperate need of some unfairly warranted police brutality?"

"Yes, officer, I've been a very naughty boy," Lester replied, barely containing his excitement as he sprinted towards Matty's bedroom, his mind racing with thoughts of the magic of Matty's marvelous, mushy mouth.

Nineteen

Officer Harrison crept from Matty's room. The early morning sunlight shining in through an open window illuminating the spitty Fixodent-stained front of his trousers, leaving no doubt as to the nature of his evening activities. He couldn't help but smile at the memory of Matty's toothless, yet enthusiastic oral session.

Leaning over the stairwell banister, Jacob, who had come home late the previous night with Kyle and Michael, began chanting with a mischievous grin plastered across his face. He felt odd being so joyous, but he knew that's what Nathaniel would have wanted; for them to keep living, rather than sobbing and wallowing. He chanted louder, his voice echoed through the house with the flair of a ringmaster introducing a circus act as he caught Officer Harrison skulking toward the front door. "Shame, shame, we know your name!"

"Shhhh!" Lester whispered, putting a finger to his lips in an attempt to silence the boy, but it was already too late. Drawn by their brother's boisterous tune, Kyle and Michael exited their room and peered over the banister at the red-faced officer while Lucas and Misty wandered in from the kitchen.

Mortified, Lester attempted to shake off the boys' taunting. "Ummm... Mornin' son. I... uh... interrogated your grandma and her story checks out. Looks like everything here is on the up-and-up."

At that moment, Matty emerged from her room, the little hair she had remaining on her head resembling a bird's nest after a night of harsh 'interrogation.' Wrapped in a threadbare muumuu through which her drooping breast could clearly be seen, she sauntered up behind Officer Harrison and gave his rear a playful smack, then fished around in a pocket of her robe. Triumphant, she withdrew her lint-encrusted dentures and popped them into her mouth.

The sight of this sent the group into fits of giggles, their laughter echoing through the room. Harrison, caught in the crossfire of their gleeful gazes, tried to pull a disappearing act, shrinking further into his own skin.

"Don't forget these, big boy," Matty quipped, fishing out a pair of handcuffs from the depths of the other pocket, her cataract-coated eyes twinkling with mischief.

"Ma," Misty sighed, shaking her head in disapproval.

Unfazed, Matty sauntered around Officer Harrison to stand in front of him. "So, you'll be joining us for dinner tonight, right?"

"Um... Sure..." Lester replied, his voice a mix of resignation and anticipation.

"Great! Now, pucker up." Matty swiftly removed her dentures and planted her lips, still carrying the aroma of morning breath, onto his. Her tongue, like a slime-coated Hagfish, pushed its way into his mouth.

Harrison, caught between arousal and embarrassment, returned the kiss hastily then bid the family farewell, making his exit as quickly as possible. Discreetly trying to adjust the sticky hardon tenting the front of his khaki uniform pants.

Twenty

After dispatching Lucas to the market to fetch the sides for tonight's feast and telling Michael to install a padlock on the basement door—the hiding spot for the 'meat'—to keep their new housemate from snooping until he got accustomed to their lifestyle, Matty was busy in the kitchen whipping up an Agape Feast. The pièce de résistance? A generous serving of Reverend Tumblin, sliced and diced. Which she thought rather fitting for the traditional communal meal that brought together Christians from every social class.

Misty was certain that both Lucas and Lester were privy to the Collins's peculiar penchant for flesh, but thought it better to err on the side of caution until the gory details were ironed out.

Matty limped into the kitchen and took a deep breath. "Smells edible!" she exclaimed as she plopped down at the breakfast table.

"You think Frank's gonna grace us with his presence tonight?" Misty asked, her voice tinged with anxiety.

"Reckon so," Matty replied casually.

"What the hell are we gonna do? The exorcism was a flop, and we can't even lay a finger on him. He's already knocked off Nathaniel and Reverend Tumblin. At this rate, the rest of the family's gonna be toast by the weekend."

"Girly, if I knew, I'd tell ya. Guess we just gotta wait and see what old Frankie boy has up his sleeve the next time he makes an appearance, and deal with his antics one catastrophe at a time."

The rest of the day drifted by in a fog as Matty busied herself with dinner preparations. Lucas returned with enough groceries to open a small convenience store, and soon after, the rest of the motley crew—Michael, Jacob, and Kyle—sauntered in. They were followed by an attractive but rather disheveled girl around 20, who wore cut-off jeans short enough to moonlight as swimsuit bottoms and a crop top showing enough under-boob that the bottom of her nipples were playing peek-aboo.

"This here is Courtney," Kyle said with a casual wave of her hand. "Picked her up hitchhiking down the road. She looked a bit peckish so figured I'd invite her to dinner before giving her a ride to the next town."

Misty glanced at Matty, then Kyle, and offered the newcomer a smile.

"It's nice to meet you, Courtney. Feel free to freshen up a bit. The bathroom is down the hall, first door on the left. Dinner will be ready shortly."

Courtney flashed a grin as wide as a Cheshire cat and said, "Thanks a heap, ma'am! I've been hitchhiking my way to Hollywood, aiming to become one of them big movie stars. It's been a few days since I had anything that resembles food, so I really appreciate the grub." With that, Courtney sashayed off to freshen up, leaving Misty to elbow Kyle, who was practically puddling the floor with drool as she watched Courtney's departure.

"Girl, have you completely lost your marbles?" Misty whispered once Courtney was out of earshot.

"What, ma! Micheal gets to parade his boyfriend around at dinner, and I'm barred from bringing a date? It's downright unjust."

"What!" Michael exclaimed, mortified. "Lucas and I aren't boyfriends."

"Maybe not yet, but given all the thumping and moaning coming from your room last night, you're definitely booty-buddies."

"Shut up, Kyle," Michael said, shooting his sister a look sharp enough to kill.

"When can I invite someone over for dinner?" Jacob inquired, his head cocked to one side.

Kyle snorted, her eyes gleaming with a mischievous sparkle. "Bro, you're still a virgin. You've got to find someone to pop your cherry first," she teased, her voice dripping with playful sarcasm as she leaned back, arms crossed with a knowing smirk on her lips.

"MOM!" Jacob whined, his face turning the shade of a ripe tomato.

"That's enough!" Matty declared, her voice cutting through the chaos like a hot knife through butter.

"Kyle, you really think this is the best time to invite someone over? Who knows when your father might crawl out of his hidey-hole again?" Misty asked.

Kyle shrugged, brushing it off, and the conversation fizzled out as they heard Courtney making her way back from the restroom.

Shortly before 8 p.m., there was a knock at the door. Officer Harrison, still wearing his uniform, showed up with a bottle of Boone's Farm Strawberry Hill Wine in hand. He knew it was Matty's favorite, mainly because it was cheaper than therapy. Matty, having swapped out her see-through muumuu for her most fashionable, least rodent-chewed one, greeted him at the door with an alluring, toothless smile

"Oh Matty, you look...interesting," Lester commented, his tone a curious blend of uncertainty and arousal.

"Lester, you sure know how to make a girl's panties moist, now don't you? Come on in. Dinner's just about ready. She took him by the hand and led him into the dining room where Misty and Kyle were busy setting the table. Another 20 minutes found the crew seated around the table with mountains of food in front of them.

"This looks amazing!" Kyle said.

"Well, dig in," Misty encouraged.

Twenty-One

The group obliged with wide eyes and growling stomachs, their utensils clinking against the plates as they served themselves generous portions. As they savored the meal, the conversation drifted over unremarkable topics.

"Misty," Officer Harrison began between bites, "this…uh…meat is fantastic! What'd you marinate it in?"

"Oh, just a little bit of this and a little bit of that," Misty replied with an embarrassed grin.

The remainder of the evening went by without incident and Misty was on the verge of thinking that they'd make it through dinner unscathed when the light fixture about the dining table began to flicker wildly.

"Oh shit," Misty whispered, and before she could utter another word, up through the floorboard floated Frank's spectral form.

Courtney let out a banshee-like scream as Lester bolted upright from the table, fumbling to yank his gun from its holster The other kids scattered like cockroaches under a light.

"Freeze!" Lester barked, aiming the gun at Frank.

Matty, perched next to the officer, gave a slow, theatrical shake of her head. She stood up, casually tapping the gun's barrel downwards with a single finger. "Lester, you're one hell of a lay but about as sharp as a marble. What are you planning to do with a gun against a ghost?"

"Ghost?" Lester echoed in confusion.

"Yea, ghost," Frank drawled, his attention swiveling to Misty. "You see, this bitch stabbed me and bricked my body into the basement wall. So, instead of heading to the afterlife, I figure I'll stick around and torment her and her lousy family for all the hell they put me through."

"We put *you* through hell?" Misty shrieked, her voice reaching a pitch that could shatter glass. "How many times did you beat me bloody? I offed you in self-defense, and now you think you're due some kind of twisted justice?"

Lester glanced between Frank and Misty, then returned his gaze to Frank, who just shrugged with a nonchalant air. "Lester...can you blame me? You know how mouthy these Collins's women can be. Sometimes you gotta bop a bitch to get your point across."

While the Collins ladies could indeed be a handful, Lester didn't see that as a valid excuse for turning someone into a punching bag. He also knew Frank had one hell of a mean streak when he was alive, so it wasn't surprising to hear that Misty was on the receiving end of his anger, so to learn that Misty had offed him was like finding out water is wet. Before anyone could drop another bombshell, Courtney bolted for the front door as if there was a clearance sale on common sense.

Frank quickly turned his head toward the girl just in time to see her sprint out of the dining room, and he chased after her.

"Freeze!" Lester again called out as he and the rest of the family ran after them.

"I intend to," Frank responded, as his spectral form swiftly overtook and enveloped the escaping woman like a phantom second skin.

Courtney halted her sprint with a sudden scream as an unprecedented chill swept through her body. Hugging herself, she turned to the family, terror visible on her face. Her expression shifted from fear to agony, and she let out another scream as the icy sensation began to intensify, starting from her feet and spreading upward.

Her eyes bulged as much as her garishly painted toes, which dangled precariously over the edge of her ridiculously undersized sandals. A prickling sensation slithered up from the soles of her feet like a mischievous imp. As the tingling escalated, her toes underwent a rapid color transformation that would make a chameleon jealous—pink, blue, purple, and then black, before coating over in a thin, frosty glaze in a matter of seconds.

Courtney let out a blood-curdling scream as agony shot through her body, the nerves in her pinky toe spasming causing the frozen digit to snap off at the joint and go skittering across the hardwood floor. Disbelief and terror gripped her as she tried to flee from the bone-chilling cold that crept ever higher. Her sobs echoed through the room, each one more frantic than the last.

She lifted a foot, which had been frozen solid through excruciating effort, her muscles taut and straining against the biting cold that had seeped deep into her bones.

Taking a single step forward, her foot met the ground with a heavy thud, and in an instant, it shattered into a thousand glimmering shards. The fragments sparkled, catching the dim light as they skittered away, each piece reflecting the harsh reality of her struggle against the relentless freeze.

With a blood-curdling scream that echoed through the room, Courtney collapsed to the floor. The impact sent shockwaves through her body and her left foot, driven by the effect of her body hitting the floor followed suit and shattered, like a fragile crystal vase being hit by a sledgehammer. Shards of crystallized flesh exploded in every direction.

As the biting, icy cold pressed on with its relentless assault, an all-encompassing numbness seized the girl's lower extremities. A profound sense of heaviness and lethargy settled over her, making her legs feel as if they were anchored in place, practically immobile. A scream, raw and piercing enough to wake the dead, erupted from Courtney as panic surged through her veins. She realized, with chilling clarity, that she was helpless against the unforgiving embrace of Frank's phantom chill.

A jolt of icy agony surged from her thigh to her chest, sending waves of freezing pain throughout her body. She let out another piercing scream, twisting her hips in a desperate attempt to escape the torment. Her left leg, heavy and unyielding, crashed to the floor with a sickening thud. Her eyes widened in horror as her left knee shatter upon impact. In the same moment, the lower half of the same leg snapped off, brittle and fragile like a dead tree branch breaking under the weight of a winter's chill.

The pain surged in brutal, dizzying waves as the icy grip clawed its way mercilessly up her body, past her hips, immobilizing her lower half in a heartbeat.

As Frank's supernatural cold advanced ever higher, Courtney, whose screams had torn through the air without stop, felt her eyes widen in sheer horror when the acid in her stomach solidified into a frigid, immovable block. Her once fierce screams dissolved into pitiful, ragged moans as the relentless chill seized her diaphragm, each breath a jagged, agonizing battle. Her heart raced, a desperate, erratic rebellion against the invasive, icy force threatening to obliterate her body. And though Courtney realized she stood little to no chance of surviving the ghostly encounter, her body instinctively fought back. Adrenaline surged through her unfrozen veins in a frantic bid for self-preservation

The tears that escaped from Courtney's eyes froze instantly in the relentless, biting cold as an unexpected wave of serenity washed over her. It carried with it a numbness akin to anesthesia, dulling the agonizing pain that consumed her. Just as she teetered on the edge of slipping into the comforting abyss of darkness, Frank's spectral form, still possessing Kyle's unsuspecting dinner guest, surged upwards from the ground with a ghostly force, dragging Courtney with him into the air.

"Dad, don't!" Kyle screamed, her voice cracking with desperation, but Frank was unstoppable now, a force of supernatural determination.

As he and Courtney hovered mere inches below the second-floor ceiling, Frank detached himself from the dying girl, sending her plummeting towards the unforgiving ground. Courtney had a fleeting 0.64 of a second to comprehend the impending catastrophe before she crashed into the floor, whereupon everything below her diaphragm splintered into a thousand jagged fragments.

Kyle's scream pierced the air as Courtney's upper half skidded to a gruesome stop at her feet. Her eyes widened in horror as she looked down upon the tangle of crimson-stained, half-frozen bones, organs, and blood vessels. It was as if she were gazing into the depths of a grotesque yet oddly beautiful geode, Courtney's jagged insides glistened with an unnerving allure.

She glanced around the room, which was littered with fragments of Courtney's body, each piece preserved with chilling clarity—a grim testament to the efficiency of Frank's flash freezing. Her hand found its place on her hip as she looked up to Frank in anger, who hovered in the center of the room, surveying the chaotic scene with the self-satisfied air of a prideful peacock, delighting in the macabre spectacle he had orchestrated.

All she could think was how another one of her girls had been stolen from her wonderland. She couldn't believe it! Rage boiled under skin as shards of Courtney's once perfect flesh scattered around her. Standing before Frank, she spat at the ghost. Her wad sailed through him, splatting to the dirt.

"Seriously, Dad, what the fuck?"

"Oh, quit the dramatics. She wasn't even your type," Frank shot back with a smirk. "Now, who's on the chopping block next?" His gaze settled on Grandma Matty. Lester positioned himself between the spiteful spirit and his cherished Matty, puffing out his chest as if the macho display would achieve anything.

"You keep your ghostly hands off her!" Lester barked, trying to look more formidable than his wobbly knees suggested.

"Alright, have it your way. I'll tackle the pig first, then I'll deal with the hag."

Twenty-Two

"ENOUGH!" THUNDERED A VOICE that seemed to resonate from the very walls and air itself, shaking the room with a powerful presence. Suddenly, Reverend Tumblin's ghost floated up through the floorboards, ascending from the basement. The audience gawked, mouths agape.

"Really, everyone here has had just about enough of your nonsense," the reverend announced, floating over to join the equally flabbergasted specter of Frank, who looked like he had just seen a ghost... Which he had.

Frank regained his composure. "Oh yeah...? And what exactly are you gonna do about it? I mean, I ain't never met another ghost before, so got no clue if you can actually hurt me. But even if you can, you seriously think your lily-white ghost ass stands a snowball's chance in hell against me?"

"Maybe not, but I'm not here to engage in some spectral smackdown," the reverend replied with a ghostly shrug.

"So why don't you just take a one-way express ticket to Heaven, huh? Maybe after enough repenting, you'll come back as a straight guy in your next life," Frank sneered with biting sarcasm.

"Oh honey, me, a breeder? I'd rather not. I'm far too fabulous for that," came the reverend's flamboyant reply.

"Then what's your excuse for showing up here?" Frank inquired as Tumblin came to a dramatic stop, hovering beside Frank.

The reverend leaned over and murmured something into Frank's ear. Slowly, like a sunrise over a graveyard, a massive grin crept across Frank's face. When their cryptic exchange concluded, Frank, with his phantom trousers looking suspiciously snug in the crotch, turned to the crowd.

"Welp, it looks like everyone's off the hook. You're all free to go. I'll not be bothering you good folks anymore."

"What? Why?" Misty blurted out, stunned, though she wasn't exactly mourning the loss of the old Frank.

"Ummm... Reverend Tumblin has graciously agreed to assist me in atoning for my rather reckless antics from when I was alive, you know, to ensure I can finally move on to whatever afterlife has in store. But first, I need to spill all my ghostly guts and confess my sins to him. And let me tell you, I've got a laundry list of sins to confess."

"But Frank, didn't you mention you were always on your knees gazing up at the reverend in the confessional booth?" Misty asked, her face a mix of confusion and suppressed laughter.

Frank, if it were possible for a ghost, turned a shade resembling a spectral blush. "Yeah, I did say that, but I never mentioned not enjoying the view," Frank admitted, grinning sheepishly.

"So, you're saying you're..." Her voice drifted away like a balloon with a slow leak as the puzzle pieces clicked into place. All those heated debates, the shouting matches, and Frank's impressive collection of empty liquor bottles were because he was playing hide and seek with his true self all this time.

"Yes, Misty. I'm gay," Frank announced with a flourish, draping an arm around Reverend Tumblin's shoulder as if presenting the grand prize on a game show. "Sorry for the years of deception, but it's time for me to live my truth. I'm here, I'm queer, get used to it!"

Misty grinned at Frank, her expression a mix of amusement and relief. Frank grinned back, feeling like a weight had been lifted. The reverend, caught in the middle like an awkward third wheel, smiled at them both, and without needing to say anything further, all was forgiven.

"One last thing," Reverend Tumblin said. "Considering that Frank and I both passed away in the house and our spirits are trapped here, I believe it would be beneficial for the rest of you to read this."

In front of Misty, a book began to appear. Misty took hold of it as it materialized and read the title, "*The Living and the Dead. Harmonious lifestyles and peaceful co-existence. From the author of Handbook for the Recently Deceased.*"

"The thing reads like stereo instructions, but I think it'll come in handy. Eventually," Tumblin said.

"Well, we'll be going now," Frank declared, flashing a grin that could light up a graveyard. "Catch ya later." With those words, both he and Reverend Tumblin started to dissolve like sugar in coffee. The crowd let out a collective, "Awwww", as Tumblin turned and planted a spectral smooch on Frank's lips, just before they vanished from view.

Twenty-Three

"Well, this has been quite the night from hell," Matty remarked with a sardonic grin. "I don't know about y'all, but all this uproar's left me famished. Let's get these chunks of Courtney into the deep freeze before they start to thaw." She shot a glance at Lester. "Now that you're in on our little family secret, are you planning on cuffing me?"

Lester chuckled, wrapping an arm around Matty's wrinkled waist. "Maybe later," he replied with a mischievous wink.

The room erupted in groans when Matty removed her dentures, pressed her cracked lips against Lester's, and slipped her wriggling tongue into his mouth like a nightcrawler finding its way home.

Michael glanced over at Lucas with a smirk. "You good?"

Lucas chuckled darkly. "Good? I haven't had this much fun since Reverend Tumblin chaperoned Christian Camp last summer."

Misty noticed Kyle sulking and beckoned her over. "Awww, come here, sweetheart," she said, enveloping her daughter in a comforting embrace. "Don't lose sleep over Courtney. You'll meet someone new, and when you do, we'll welcome her with open arms."

Jacob, eager not to miss out, darted across the room, nearly slipping on a stray piece of Courtney, and wrapped his arms around his mom and sister.

Kyle let out a resigned sigh before breaking into a smile. "Yeah, I know."

With Frank's theatrics finally behind them, the ragtag group, now one big happy—albeit slightly twisted—family began the clean-up operation. Once Courtney had been neatly packed away in the deep freeze, they all sat down to finish the Agape Feast. After all, nothing says family lovin' like Reverend Tumblin fresh from the oven.

SOLO MISSION

MICHAEL R. COLLINS

Twenty-Four

Jacob Collins said, "To hell with it," and got out of bed. Tonight he wasn't getting any sleep. Michael was testing the bedsprings with Lucas, Kyle was downstairs in her Wonderland, Momma was in her room with God knows who, and the sounds coming from Grandma Matty's room were scary and disgusting.

Sitting on his bed in his tighty-whities, he wiped sweat from his brow. Even in the middle of the night, the air was thick and sticky. Between the insufferable heat and the inescapable sounds of the house, sleep wasn't happening. Thirsty, he wandered to the kitchen to get a drink of water.

"Goddammit. Even the fucking ghosts are at it tonight," he grumbled. The spectral image of his father, Frank, sat on the edge of the kitchen table. The equally ephemeral Reverend Tumblin's head bobbed in Frank's lap.

"Little fuckin' privacy?" Frank barked at him. "Thought you were asleep."

"Who can sleep when it's this damn hot and everyone is balls deep in everyone else?" Jacob shot back. The Honorable Reverend Tumblin didn't even bother stopping. Jacob got his drink of water and went back to his bedroom, wondering how a dead man with no saliva could still give such a sloppy sounding blowjob.

Back in his room, he reached under the bed, pulled out a shoebox, and held it with reverence. He opened it to reveal a large hunting knife. He wrapped his hand around the zebrawood handle and held it up, drinking in its chill touch and the sharp edge of its blade. It was beautiful. Their family was poor, without a doubt, and none of them had much in the way of nice things, but to him this was better than a million dollars. It was his prized possession and cared for it deeply. Maybe it was love, but maybe not.

Love was a subject he didn't know much about, and despite the activities going on in the house, it left him a little confused.

"If they don't shut up, then we can shut them up," a voice said.

"Remy, they're family. We ain't slittin' necks of family. You know that."

"But I like slitting necks. It's my favorite thing," Remy the knife replied.

"I thought your favorite thing is cutting off balls?" Jacob teased. He knew Remy liked to cut anything and anyone. He and Remy had been partners for a couple of years now. Remy never missed a hunting trip with Jacob since Michael gifted him the chatty thing. Jacob didn't ask where he got it, appreciating the gift for what it was instead.

"That was last week. I'm allowed to change my mind."

"I suppose you are." Jacob laughed. He stood and walked out with Remy in hand. Maybe it'd be cooler and quieter outside. He was right on both counts. The air, though still warm and humid, wasn't as stifling as inside. As he took a seat on his favorite stump, the only sound was that of the horny music of the insects. Out on a stump, still in his underwear, he cradled Remy. The two talked for some time before the house quieted enough for him to return.

Twenty-Five

The next morning, the family was busy. Misty and Kyle were doing the monthly deep clean of the meat locker while Michael and Lucas were burning trash. Granny and the sheriff sat on the front porch, micromanaging everyone. Jacob was in charge of floors and carpets, a job he'd hated since he'd been a little kid. He rushed to finish early so he could sneak off to hang out with his friend, Geri.

Jacob didn't have a lot of friends, but the same could be said for the rest of the family. They kept to themselves for the most part, or people avoided them at all costs. Either way, it suited them just fine, but it was nice to spend time away from the people you were related to once in a while.

Geri was as much a tomboy as Kyle, though the two were about as opposite as you could be. While Kyle can and would whoop anyone's ass at a moment's notice, Geri tried to avoid confrontation if she could help it. Though if you were unlucky enough to cross that line, she'd beat you up, down, and sideways. Jacob had seen it happen on a few rare occasions. Like the time Tanya Boothe filled the inside of Geri's new gym shoes with wads of chewed bubblegum. Geri's folks couldn't afford new ones, and Geri gave Tanya the chance to apologize and offer to buy new shoes. Tanya refused, and Geri was willing to let it be. When Tanya decided to make fun of Geri's family for being poor, it took two teachers and Jacob to pull her off the snotty little shit.

"I liked your hair longer, just saying," Jacob said, teasing her about her new haircut as they walked together. Geri's brown hair usually went down to the middle of her back, but was now chopped into a short pixie cut. Jacob actually thought it suited her.

"Too fucking hot for that," she said, wiping sweat from her brow. The fierce humidity of the early afternoon even had the bugs too bothered to make much noise. They walked down the road, keeping on the dirt shoulder. The road didn't see much traffic except by farmers or people who got lost coming off the highway. "So what all's been going on at your house? I've been hearing all sorts of wild things. Why is old man Harrison spending so much time there? Last place I'd expect him."

"He and Granny are bumping uglies. Ever since that woman got out of the institution, it's been crazy. Daddy came back to haunt us, and now he and the ghost of Rev Tumblin are fucking up a storm at all hours. Lucas and Michael are doing the same."

"Sounds like a damn orgy house." Geri laughed, nudging him with her elbow. "You must hate it."

"I ain't sleeping much, that shit is for sure," Jacob grumbled.

Geri laughed again, then stopped mid-chuckle. "What did you mean about your daddy's ghost and the reverend?"

"I don't want to get into it. It's a long story." Jacob gave a dismissive wave.

"Fair enough. But if you ever feel like finally getting your dick wet, my offer still stands. Harriet Glensbury still has the hots for you. All I gotta do is make a call, and she'll land right on your lap," Geri teased.

"Harriet Glensbury collects STDs like your momma collects those weird little porcelain dolls. And besides, I'm not as interested in that as the rest of my horndog family."

"Suit yourself." Geri shrugged. She slipped off the brown plaid shirt she was wearing over her tank top. They passed by the Redfield home as she did. Burl Redfield stood by his barn and watched them as they passed. His eyes were glued to Geri as she tied the shirt around her waist. More specifically, he was staring at her small breasts and long legs.

"Hey girl, leave that white trash you're walking with and come over here for a minute? Got an offer for you," Burl called to her.

He was shirtless under her overalls, his massive gut stretching the worn denim to its limit.

"If you're trying to offer me that micropenis of yours, you'd be better off catching a flying fuck," Geri called back without hesitation.

"Better than anything you're getting from those Collins reprobates." Burl nodded at Jacob.

"Last I heard, Dottie Stevens had to call on the search and rescue team to find your hard on." Jacob shot back. Dottie Stevens was the town prostitute. Nice lady, even if she did have a few miles on her. Granny claimed she was turning tricks even back when she was still little. And that was at least a hundred years ago, Jacob thought.

"It ain't the size that counts!" Burl hollered as the two friends walked away.

"Whoever told you that was trying not to hurt your feelings!" Geri cackled.

The Redfields and the Collins's were as far from friends and two families could get. Rumor was the bad blood began when Jacob's great-grandpa tried to buy some pasture from Burl's father. The old man called Great-Grandpa everything but a child of God and shooed him off the porch with a shotgun. Since then, relations between the two families had been chilly at best. Granny and Burl's wife, Patty, hated each other something fierce. No one was sure what happened between the two, but neither could be in the same room with each other for more than a minute. Longer than that, cops and EMTs were called to the scene. The fact that the families lived less than a mile from each other didn't help ease tensions either.

As the two friends cleared the Redfield's property line, Jacob looked over his shoulder. Burl's grandson leaned against a fence post leering at Geri. He had a hand in his pocket, and the way he was moving it around in there, he either was trying to fish some change out, or playing with himself. Jacob doubted Jimbo had a penny to his name, so he nudged Geri, and they walked away faster.

Twenty-Six

"That Jimbo Redfield is on my last fuckin' nerve." Kyle stormed into the house. "He lays hands on me one more time, he's going to lose 'em." Her complaining stopped the moment she saw the sheriff, his head slumped on the table and a pool of blood under his seat. She looked at Michael, who leaned against the sink, drinking a soda as he waited for Lucas to return from running a few errands.

"Grandma," Michael informed her, then burped.

"It was only a matter of time." Kyle shook her head. "Fine, I guess I can take my frustrations out on him instead. You boys want to help me get him downstairs?"

"He ain't for eating," Misty said, entering the kitchen behind her daughter. "Momma's orders."

"Shit, he must have pissed her off good." Kyle peeked under the table at the red pool. "She shoot his dick off?" Her brother nodded an affirmative. Kyle whistled. "He fucked up bad, then."

"Great, another ghost." Misty shook her head. "Last thing we need right now."

"He'll keep his dead ass away if he knows what's good for him," Grandma Matty said, stomping down the stairs. She disappeared into the living room and out the front door to sit in her rocker on the porch.

"What's that science-experiment reject done now?" Michael asked, handing his soda to Kyle. She took a swig from it, burped long and loud.

"He got all handsy with me. He keeps inviting me into his barn for a 'roll in the hay', said he had some other girl there and wanted a threesome. Even if I *were* interested in swinging his way, it sure wouldn't be with that disgusting creep. The only way he could get a threesome is with two inflatable dolls." She took another swig and held the can out to Michael.

Jacob walked into the kitchen, took the can, guzzled it, belched, then handed the empty back to Michael. Michael glared at them both and tossed the can in the trash.

"We had a run-in with Ol' Burl this morning. He was giving Geri a bad time," Jacob said, then looked over at the sheriff. "Granny?" They all nodded. "I'll give you a hand, Kyle."

"Nope. He ain't for eating," Kyle said. "We ain't letting him sit here and rot, right? This is where we eat."

Misty shook her head and pointed over her shoulder out the back door.

"I'll get the shovels." Jacob sighed. Michael followed behind, a fresh soda in hand. As he passed his momma, she took it from him and guzzled it herself. Michael swore as he walked outside.

"Cut his head off and bury it somewhere else. If he comes back as a ghost, I want him to have to look for it," Granny hollered from the porch.

The brothers threw the shovels into the van and went back for the body. Outside, Michael took the axe that was leaning against the house and with a quick chop, separated head and body. He and Jacob kicked it like a soccer ball to the van.

"You think Jimbo got a girl for a threesome? He's more full of shit than a politician's outhouse, but he ain't one to take no for an answer either," Jacob said to Kyle as he leaned against the van. He thought about Geri and their encounter earlier in the day. It wasn't the first time Jimbo or Burl had harassed her. It didn't help that Jimbo had been accused of rape on more than one occasion.

"That Burl is a mean sonofabitch and so is that cunt wife of his," Granny said as she walked out the back door, checking on her grandchildren's progress. "The only one who was worth a shit was their son Vern, and even he was only worth a small turd at best. Best thing Vern ever did was die early. Shame he had to get the Turley girl pregnant with that waste of semen son of his, Jimbo."

She shooed Kyle off the step so she could sit down. Kyle hopped up without protest, knowing Granny was still in a bad mood. "Burl raising his grandson Jimbo just made a bad situation worse. The best thing that can happen is the whole Redfield clan gets fed into a wood chipper."

Jacob, Michael, and Kyle all exchanged glances. "Well...we can always—" Michael started before Granny cut him off.

"Oh no, we'd be first on the list of suspects. No, just leave them assholes alone. Now, it's getting late. Kyle, be useful for once and help your momma with supper." Granny stood and walked into the house. Kyle waited until her back was turned to flip her double birds. From inside the house, Granny called out, "I saw that, girl."

"You're dead meat now." Jacob laughed. Kyle hung her head as she trudged into the house. Michael and Jacob got in the van to dispose of Officer Harrison. Jacob couldn't shake the nagging feeling about Jimbo wanting a threesome. There had been some stories about the goings-on in Redfield's barn, and while none of them were surprising, he paid little attention. Neither Burl nor Jimbo took the word 'no' seriously. In fact, they took it damned personal.

He knew he shouldn't worry about Geri; she was tough. But the Redfields were bigger, even if most of their bulk was mostly flab. "Shit," he muttered, hoping he was worrying over nothing. Maybe because he was still tired from getting no sleep last night, but he had to check and make sure she wasn't in their barn.

"Hold on a sec," he told his older brother. He went inside and grabbed the phone off the kitchen wall. Ducking around the corner with it, he dialed Geri's parents' house. Her mother answered, saying that Geri hadn't been home since that morning. Jacob hung up, worried. Something wasn't right.

"I gotta go check on something; you got this, right?" Jacob asked Michael as he trotted toward the Redfield's house. Michael swore as he watched Jacob go. He always got stuck with the shit jobs.

Jacob had nearly made it to Burl's property line before he realized he should have grabbed Remy. The knife would call him a fool later and tease him for thinking Geri couldn't handle herself, but he was used to that. Going unarmed felt like a bad idea, but he wasn't planning on confronting anyone if he could help it.

The sun was getting low, and the fields were orange by the time Jacob came up on the Redfield's barn. He heard two voices inside. Both sounded excited and out of breath. With all the stealth he had developed from hunting, he crept up to the dusty window along the barn wall and peered inside. He blinked, making sure what he saw was correct. As he realized what he was seeing, rage filled him from his toes to the top of his head.

Geri lay discarded in a pile of musty hay. Her pants were down around her ankles, and her tank top ripped open. She was motionless, her lifeless eyes staring at nothing. Blood streaked her face and crotch. Burl stood over the body, examining her. His pot belly hanging over his soft, stubby prick. Jimbo had his pants up, but his shirt off. He was on his way to resembling his rotund grandfather.

"Afraid we might have taken it a little too far with her," Burl drawled.

"Don't we always?" Jimbo guffawed. His donkey laugh set Jacob's nerves on edge. If he'd had Remy, he'd have gutted the two of them right now. It took everything he had not to break through this window and rip them apart with his bare hands. The shotgun he saw leaning against the wall helped him keep his resolve. Most likely, they had it to keep Geri in line as well. Otherwise, she'd done some damage to them both before running away.

"We do, don't we." Burl joined his son's laughter. "They're just women. More where they came from. C'mon, let's get a beer. We've built up a thirst." The older man bent over to pull up his overalls, giving Jacob a shot of his ass. Clearly wiping well wasn't a priority for him, given the dried brown smear crusting around his flabby ass-crack. Jacob wanted to puke.

"Don't let Grandma catch you talking like that about women," Jimbo said, still staring at Geri.

"Sheeeit. Your Grandmomma got the same attitude I do about them. How'd you think we wound up with her? She went and rounded her up for us." Burl kicked Geri's leg. "Let's get cleaned up for dinner. We'll get her buried in the morning. She ain't going anywhere." With another sharp laugh, the two exited the barn.

Jacob's anger was so intense it left him immobile. He wanted to tear them limb from limb. He wanted to drag the entire family through glass and razor blades before tossing them into the septic tank. After letting them soak in the filth, he'd fish them out, lay them on a fire ant hill. Let the ants and sepsis kill them slowly. Let the pain take a good long time. He didn't want death; he wanted prolonged agony.

When he was able to move again, he backed away from the barn as quietly as he came upon it. He needed Remy. Remy would know what to do. Remy always did.

Twenty-Seven

Jacob said little during dinner. He ate, put his plate in the sink, and went to his room. Granny threatened to cut his pecker off if he didn't sit his ass down and wait to be excused, but he ignored her. Truth is, he barely even heard her. His thoughts were full of revenge and blood.

In his room, he shut his door and brought Remy out. He explained what he saw and what he had in mind. Remy said nothing. This worried Jacob. There was a time when Remy didn't talk to him. They had a fight, Jacob accusing Remy of trying to manipulate him, Remy accusing Jacob of being too dumb to know his ass from a hole in the ground. Eventually they made up, but Jacob hated the silence in between.

"Remy, what do you think? You ready to cut them Redfield fuckers up into the smallest pieces imaginable?" Jacob asked for a second time, hoping for a response.

After a long minute, Remy said, "You know how much I like to cut fuckers up into the smallest pieces imaginable. That's a given. But we may have to handle this in a more delicate fashion."

"Delicate? I want pain and revenge, not to be dainty about it," Jacob hissed, anger dripping from every word.

"Delicate doesn't always mean dainty, idiot." Remy shot back. "We go there just cutting them all up, they'll assume it was us. We'll have to get creative. Make it look like anyone could have done it. I mean, they've done a lot of bad to a lot of people, right?"

"Creative won't be a problem. Between Michael, Kyle, and me, we can come up with something. Shoot, even Lucas has some good ideas now and again," Jacob said. Behind him, he heard footsteps in the hallway stop at his door. After a moment, the footsteps went away.

"No. You have to do this alone. Getting the family involved will only make it more of a production than it has to be. Plus, those two siblings of yours are about as subtle as a bass drum. Michael is a great hunter but not terribly imaginative, and Kyle only does her best work when she's horny."

"I don't like keeping things from the family. But I guess you're right. Plus Granny didn't want us messing with them to begin with. What do you suggest?" While he didn't exactly agree with

Remy's assessment of his brother and sister, he understood the sentiments. But it still didn't help him. If Remy wasn't willing to do the cutting, then how was he getting revenge over Geri?

"First off, you're going to get your friend's body and bury her somewhere nice. Maybe down by the creek where you two used to hang out as kids. Then you're going to do *your* thing. You're more than a hunter. You're imaginative, and you're going to put that imagination to work. Time to give yourself a chance to prove yourself."

"If you say so," Jacob said reluctantly.

Down in the kitchen, Grandma turned to her daughter, Misty. "That boy Jacob ain't right. He's in his room murmuring with someone, and I know he didn't sneak anyone in this house. He's in there talking to himself, I think."

"Leave him alone. He's just fine. Being a middle child is hard enough." Misty stubbed out her cigarette in the ashtray. She knew Jacob had some imaginary friends when he was young, but she'd hoped he'd grown out of them by now.

"If it was so damn tough to be a middle child, then get rid of the others. Worked for me," Granny griped.

Twenty-Eight

Jacob did as Remy suggested and snuck out of the house, waiting for all the sex noises to start. He took Remy with him this time. To ensure no one heard him, he pushed the van out of the driveway and onto the road before starting it up and heading to the Redfield's farm. He snuck into the barn, making sure no lights were on in the rundown farmhouse first. True to their word, they left Geri's body there in the hay, waiting until morning to dispose of it. Mostly likely to the pigs out back.

Rage swelled in Jacob again, and Remy had to talk him back down. He picked up a nearby can of gasoline, ready to burn the house down with everyone in it, but Remy convinced him that there were better ways to go about his revenge. Still pissed, but unwilling to argue, he carefully carried Geri to the van.

Taking the back roads to Brite Creek, he found a spot in the trees and buried her deep. He didn't feel right not giving her body back to her momma. She would worry about her girl and call the police. Since the remaining local police who hadn't been killed at the Collins house were practically incompetent, it would take forever for them do anything worth a shit. Burl and Jimbo would most likely get off scot-free, like always, and go after Geri's momma in retaliation.

Revenge was more important and the best course of action. Once all was said and done, he'd let her momma know what happened and where she was. It would be better off, anyway. Her momma was too poor to afford a funeral. This spot by the creek was a much prettier place to be buried than the weed-infested cemetery outside of town. Here, she could visit her daughter surrounded by beauty. Jacob promised himself to see about getting something nice to mark the grave with.

After he had finished, Jacob sat by the creek and listened to it in the dark. The black water rushed by, and he considered what he wanted to do to ease his anger. When the sky started to turn a light purple, he drove home before anyone noticed the van was gone. He was ready to go because he had a plan. On the drive home, he explained it to Remy.

"Told you there was an imagination in there," Remy exclaimed happily. "This one is all you."

Twenty-Nine

Two days passed. Granny almost derailed the entire operation when she went into town and got into a fight with Patty Redfield at the market. Neither could be in the same building together without violence happening.

"That festering twat is a waste of space. You should send the boys over there tonight. We'd eat for weeks on them fat asses," Granny hissed.

"We'd die of high cholesterol, more like it." Lucas giggled.

"What happened between you and Patty, anyway?" Misty asked. "You two been at each other for as long as I can remember. Wasn't she the one who paid the editor of the paper to run a public service announcement announcing you were a health hazard because you had syphilis?"

Everyone's face grew red as they held in their giggles. Granny slapped the table. "That bitch thought she got the last laugh, but I got even. I told my cousin Lurlene to sleep with Burl. Lurlene had a case of gonorrhea from her Army boyfriend that could burn a hole through plate steel. All she had to do was shake her ass at that fat bastard and he was all up in her. It didn't take too long before Burl and Patty were slinking off to the doctor to get a shot."

"I'm sure she knew it was you who set it up, though," Kyle said.

Granny snorted. "Ain't the first time we got into it. Me and Patty been at war since we was in school. It wasn't always that way though. We were running buddies for a bit. Me, her, and Bernice Chumley. Back then, the three of us were a handful. This town didn't know what hit it.

"One day, out of boredom, we decided to knock off Bordon's Drug Store. Bernice wanted some makeup, and I'm sure Patty had contracted her first case of the clap, so she needed drugs. I was just bored. We put on some men's work clothes, covered our heads with pillowcases, and I grabbed my pop's shotgun.

"Everything went great until Patty and I got into an argument about old man Bordon. She had him tied up to his office chair in the back, and he was hollering his head off, shouting our names out because I guess our reputation preceded us." Granny chuckled at that. "I wanted to blow his head off, but she didn't want to deal with the mess. Bernice was too busy loading up her bag with every cosmetic in the place.

"Being tied to that chair must have woken something up in the old man because as we were arguing, Patty noticed he had a hard on the likes of which he ain't ever had before. So we compromised. I didn't shoot him with the twelve gauge if he kept quiet. If he said anything, then we'd let the whole town know he got off on being tied up by teenage girls. He agreed to those terms provided we came back next week and did it again."

"If you two were knocking off drugstores, why do you two hate each other so much?" Michael asked.

Granny shrugged. "Oh, who can remember these things? It doesn't matter much. Stay away from them Redfields, especially you, Kyle. More than a few girls ain't ever come out of that barn."

Jacob held his tongue. The fact that the two families had a history might throw some suspicion on what he was about to do, but he'd be willing to take that chance. He was determined to go through with this, no matter what. They deserved what they were going to get.

As the morning sun peaked the horizon, Jacob took Lucas to the side as he came to breakfast. "Hey, can you show me some of those fancy knots you use on my brother?"

Lucas looked at him, impressed. "You have someone special? You sure you want your first time with complicated knots?"

"Why does everyone think I'm a virgin?" Jacob rolled his eyes.

"You're not?"

"Not important. Can you show me?" Jacob followed Lucas out back and showed him a few of his favorite knots. An hour later, Jacob was ready. When evening came, he'd be ready to strike. He just needed one more thing.

"Hey Kyle, I need you to do me a favor," he said, catching her before she disappeared downstairs later that afternoon. He didn't know who she had down there and he didn't care. They could wait. "I need you to call over at the Redfield's and ask for Jimbo. Tell him you wanna meet up with him for sex."

"Ew! No! What the hell?" Kyle recoiled.

"You don't have to go through with it. I just need you to say it," Jacob explained.

"I don't want to meet up with him even if we don't have sex."

Jacob sighed. "You don't have to meet up with him at all. Just call and tell him you'll meet him for sex, but he better hurry. Steal his pa's truck if he has to. Those exact words."

Kyle examined her brother for a moment. "What are you up to?"

"You'll see. I got a few things to do first." Jacob grinned. "I'll let you know when to call. Make sure he takes his pa's truck." He turned to go. "You're the best sister I have."

"I'm your only sister!" she shouted at him as he disappeared out the back door.

Thirty

Burl Redfield stumbled into his barn from the side door. He found the bottom of that liquor bottle sooner than he expected. He wasn't drunk, but he was close enough to touch it. Evening had fallen, and the shadows were long enough to almost call it a night. He came in here only because he heard crashing in the barn, so he came to investigate. He peered at the pile of bloody hay where they had left the girl's body. The body wasn't there.

That boy finally cleaned up a mess for once, Burl thought, kicking the dry hay with his shit-covered boot. His foot froze. He and his grandson had been out most of the afternoon getting groceries for dinner and liquor for him. After that, they dropped Patty off at Bingo. Burl came home, and Jimbo disappeared into his bedroom. Both of them had forgotten about the girl.

"Shit," he swore. "If Patty cleaned that bitch up for us before we left, I'll never hear the fuckin' end of it. Bet she's just waiting for me to notice."

"She had a name, you shit stain." Jacob sprang out from behind the stack of moldy hay bales he was hiding behind. With a calculated swing of the shovel, he connected with Burl's head. He didn't use all his force, just enough to knock him out. Burl fell like a sack of rocks. Jacob panicked and bent over his prone body. He could still smell rancid breath coming from his mouth, so he wasn't dead. Good, he had plans for ol' Burl.

Burl's bulk made it a herculean task to drag his body closer to the barn door. Once there, he tied one length of rope just like Lucas taught him. After the hands were tied, he worked on the feet. No matter what, these ropes couldn't come off. Not that he could just finish the job with the shovel right now and be done with it, but he wanted it done in a special way.

Outside it was getting darker and Jacob knew he was nearly out of time. Kyle was going to call any minute. The next step was to tie the rope around the front of the ancient tractor he parked there while the family was out. Luckily, Jacob had helped some of the local farmers for some extra money during harvest seasons in the past. Since most everyone was just scraping by, he had learned to drive a lot of the old beasts.

He opened the squeaky barn door enough to peer out. Jimbo was still inside. Good. It took only a second to secure the rope to the trailer hitch of Burl's old pick up which was backed up to the barn door just like it always was. Jacob prayed Burl's bulk didn't pull the frame out from under the old Ford before any damage to the old man could be done.

Inside the house the phone rang as Jacob checked his work. The rope looked obvious as hell; Jimbo, dumb as he was, would see it for sure. Jacob ran over and kicked dirt on it best he could. He closed the barn door again.

Burl's eyes fluttered as he came to. Jacob took the roll of duct tape hanging from a nail on the wall, ripped a length off, and put it over Burl's mouth before he could scream and alert his son. "This is for Geri," Jacob said, kicking him in the ribs.

A hoot of excitement rang out as Jimbo barreled out the front door. Jacob prayed that Jimbo didn't see the rope attached to the trailer hitch. The moment the truck fired up and the exhaust wafted into the barn, Burl thrashed and moaned. The rope went taut as the truck lurched forward. Jimbo, accelerator to the floor, tore down the dirt drive, too horny to care about anything else. The rope jerked tight. Burl screamed behind the silver tape. With a wet rip Burl's arms and legs came off. His arms stayed connected to the tractor as his legs slammed into the barn door, breaking through the old wooden planks and bouncing along behind the old truck.

Splattered in blood, Jacob stood there as Burl's dying moans quickly subsided. A smile crept across Jacob's face. He pulled Remy out. "You're right. I do feel better."

"One down," Remy said. Jacob smiled. Everything was working out like he'd planned so far. The Redfields had gone long enough for him to do some prep work, then Burl came to investigate the racket he raised to lure him out. He also counted on Jimbo being stupid and horny enough to steal his grandpa's truck to get with his sister.

Jacob put Remy away and stood up. He kicked Burl's bloody trunk with his foot. Satisfied, he opened the back barn door then hopped up on the tractor. As the seconds ticked by, he worried Jimbo wasn't smart enough to figure out what happened. He wondered where Kyle told him to meet her. Hopefully not far. He didn't want Patty coming home and finding her husband before Jimbo returned. While he would kill her if he needed too, his revenge plan only had reservations for two. He'd let her live with the aftermath, which now that he thought about it, was a torture all its own.

At last he heard the truck racing back towards the barn. It skidded to a halt. Jacob put his fingers on the key, ready to start the ancient tractor as Jimbo followed the blood trail and pulled open the barn door to see the torn body of his grandpa on the dirt floor.

Jimbo looked at the body, then back at the truck. The two legs were still attached to the trailer hitch, now brown with dirt. Jacob waited until realization dawned on Jimbo's face he was the one that killed the old man. A gut-wrenching howl of anguish filled the barn. Jacob chose that moment to flick the lights of the tractor on.

Jimbo lifted his arm up to shield his eyes. He swore as his eyes adjusted to the sudden brightness. He saw a smiling Jacob, covered in blood, leaning against the steering wheel. "I'll get you, you piece of white trash," Jimbo roared.

"Ha! Look who's talking." Jacob pushed in the clutch and turned the key of the old tractor. It grumbled and snorted. Jimbo closed the distance as Jacob tried again. Again nothing. He said a small prayer to the gods of International Harvester and turned the key again. With a belch of smoke it rattled to life. It protested as he put it into reverse and started backwards. He crashed through the back of the barn, Jimbo screeching again as his pa's arms raced passed him, still attached to the front of the tractor.

While the Redfield clan was out earlier in the day, Jacob attached the post hole auger to the back of the tractor and dug a deep hole fifty yards out in the field. Now, as he rumbled over the furrowed field, he approached the hole and killed the lights. A few more yards and he watched over his shoulder and saw the dark hole pass underneath him. Once he was clear, he stomped on the break. In the dark, Jimbo ran right past the hole but couldn't stop in time and bounced off the nose of the tractor. He stumbled, holding his nose. Dancing around the hole, Jacob wondered if he was going to have to just push him until Jimbo disappeared out of sight.

"What the fuck?" Jimbo yelled from the bottom of the pit. The sound of the tractor's engine covered the dusty scrambling of his attempts to crawl out.. "Why did you kill my pa?"

"Why did you have your way with Geri and then kill her?"

"You ain't going to leave me in this hole to die are you? My gramma gonna git you. She's coming home from Bingo, get me outta this hole, then kill you and your family."

"Sure she is," Jacob said. He hopped off the tractor, leaving the engine going.

"Get me outta here!" Jimbo screamed again. His voice going higher in pitch.

"Sure. Hold on." Jacob unzipped his fly and pissed in the hole. Jimbo spluttered and raged some more. "Oh, hold your horses. I'll give you a hand." He took two disembodied arms, still attached to the rope and slid them down the hole, just far enough for Jimbo to reach them. Jimbo cried out in disgust calling Jacob all the nastiest names he could think of. Whistling, Jacob climbed back up on the tractor.

"You want up, you better hold our poppa's hands," Jacob told him.

"You're the devil. You're whole family is!"

Jacob rolled his eyes, already tired of the insults. He put it into gear, grinding the old gears and slowly backed up. Jimbo told him to wait as he clambered to get hold but it was too late.

Jacob, still whistling, pulled the tractor around and backed up to the hole.

Jimbo looked up at the large auger that hovered above his head. "What... What you doin' with that?"

"This is for Geri." Jacob engaged a lever and the large auger started turning. Jimbo screamed more as Jacob put the tractor in neutral and revved the engine, drowning him out. He pulled the lever back and the auger slowly lowered into the hole. Jacob looked up at the twinkling stars as the sound of wet crunching replaced the screaming. Blood and bone flew up as the turnscrew blades cut through the young rapist with ease. Once the crunching stopped he raised the auger again and returned the tractor back into the barn. A feeling of a job well-done filled him as he walked back home. He pulled Remy out of its sheath again.

"Proud of you, kid. You did a good job," Remy said.

"Thanks. I appreciate that. I don't hear that much, so it means a lot." Jacob held Remy close. "Kinda feel bad though. You didn't get to cut nobody."

"They'll be time enough for that," Remy told him. "This one was for you."

Thirty-One

Jacob woke with a start. He had the best sleep he'd had in several nights and was looking forward to sleeping in. Instead, someone pounded on the front door and yelled enough to wake the entire county. Just as he pulled his pants on, Michael burst through his bedroom door.

"You better get down here. Patty Redfield is at the door and she's calling for blood." He picked up a dirty T-shirt and tossed it to Jacob. "This about you coming home all bloody last night? Kyle thinks you went and killed Burl and Jimbo."

Jacob gave him a knowing smile as he left his room and raced down the stairs.

"Boy! What did you do?" Misty caught Jacob by the ear. She pinched hard, pulling him into the kitchen. "Don't matter how old or how big you get. I'm still your momma. What did you do?

She's out there accusing us of murder. On our front porch no less!"

"They killed my friend Geri. I had to get back at them. Honest Momma, that's all I did."

"You know about this?" Misty turned to Michael, Lucas, and Kyle who all hung their heads and nodded. "Can't turn away from any of you for a second before you're stirring up more trouble."

"Let me in, you murdering scum!" Patty screamed at the back door. A gunshot rang out and the doorknob fell to the floor. With a kick, the kitchen door flew open and Patty's overstuffed body lumbered into the room.

"You pulled apart my Burl! Limb from limb!" Her high-pitched squeals sent Michael's finger into his ears. Lucas put his hands over his. Kyle just winced. "Then he cut my boy up in little bitty pieces with the post-hole digger. Little bitty pieces!" Spittle flew from her lips.

"What in the name of Jehovah's all holy right testicle is going on down here?!" Granny Matty raged as she came down the stairs. The moment she lay eyes on Patty she stopped in mid step. Her eyes grew hard. "Get out of my house before I shove your head so far up your ass they'll need five men and a crane to pull it out.

"Your no-good family killed my Burl and my grandson." Patty waved the gun around. The only one who seemed affected was Lucas, who was not used to being threatened with weapons.

"About time someone did. Ain't no woman safe from you animals," Granny said simply.

"They may have fooled around, but at least they didn't have sex with 'em before eating 'em." Patty's jowls shook with condemnation. Kyle looked at the floor, feeling the smirks from her brother's pointed in her direction. Granny just laughed at Patty.

"I'll kill you and your whole family!" she screamed waving the gun at each of them.

"Patty Redfield, your family's list of sins is so long it's coming out with a second edition. You also can't shoot for shit," Matty said, goading her.

"Momma, please," Misty said under her breath.

Jacob looked the kitchen table. To his surprise, Remy was still lying there. After he came home last night, he sat to have a glass of milk before bed. As the exhaustion replaced exhilaration, he didn't realize he had left the knife on the table. If only he could get to the knife in time.

"She'll blow your head off before you get to me," Remy warned. "Don't try it." Jacob heeded the warning. First chance he got, though, he'd go for it.

"Matty, you've been my nemesis since we were little. Always bullying me when we was young. I never forgave you for sleeping with my daddy."

"I'm also the one who told everyone about how you'd sneak off and let your cousin Teddy knock on your backdoor during the family reunions. And who the hell uses the word 'nemesis'?"

"FUCKING WHORE!" The roar of the rifle filled the room. Plaster rained down on Grandma's head.

"Told you she can't shoot for shit. My turn." Grandma reached for Remy and snatched the knife off the table.

"My time to shine!" Remy yelled in exultation.

"Damn straight it is," Grandma told it before letting the knife fly.

Jacob watched the knife flip through the air as if in slow motion. He stood agog, shocked that Grandma could hear Remy too.

The knife impaled Patty right in her throat, the impact forcing her back against the wall. With a gurgling cough, she slid down the wall. Blood gushed from around the knife and out her mouth. Jacob could hear little else but the muffled cheers and cries of triumph coming from the happy blade.

"Noisy bastard, ain't he?" Grandma said to Jacob and shuffled out of the room. "Clean this shit up and get some breakfast on."

"What in the fuck is going on in here? It's enough to wake the dead." Frank's spectral head popped around the corner of the doorway. From somewhere else in the house, the reverend's voice asked what he saw. He looked around, then yelled over his shoulder. "They must have got in an argument with Patty Redfield. She's got that motormouth knife in her neck." He faded away.

"You're doing all the work this time." Michael poked Jacob in the chest. He and Lucas went to get the van.

"Ain't eating this nasty bitch," Kyle said wrinkling her nose and following the others.

Jacob pulled the knife from Patty's throat. As he wiped the blood off on his pants he could hear Remy happily cooing. He set down Remy with care and took Patty's wrists, struggling to pull her bulk through the doorway.

"Lay something down before you trail blood through my house," Misty admonished him. "I swear, it's like you were all raised in the wild."

It Ain't Over 'Til It's Over

CHISTO HEALY

Thirty-Two

The End

Agent Becker lowered the binoculars, the vision of the house still lingering in his mind. "You're sure this is it?" he asked.

A younger man beside him adjusted his glasses and cleared his throat. He fixed the FBI identification on his suit and cleared his throat again. "Um, yes, sir. That's the Collins place."

Becker stuck a toothpick in his mouth. It wasn't a cigarette, but it would have to do. He needed to quit those things. Doctor said so, but even if they didn't, he knew he was too old to try to chase perps on smoker lungs. "What's their body count again?"

The younger agent scratched at the back of his neck and fixed his glasses again. "We don't know for certain, sir, but it's well over a hundred."

Becker sighed. "Christ, that's more than my ex-wife."

"Sir?"

"Never mind. Is that total with the other family or just the Collins?"

"Both, sir."

"Have we looked in on the others? Enemies or not, they may see us as a reason to unite."

The younger man nodded. "Yes, sir. Um, every member of the Redfield family is missing. We've used thermal technology, and there are no heat signatures anywhere in or below their residence. It seems like the Collins family may have already taken care of that part of the problem for us."

"Jesus." Becker spat the toothpick into the leaves at his feet and fished a cigarette from his pocket. He shoved it into his mouth and lit it before he could talk himself out of it. "Why is it always hillbillies, Brennan? You know, I've known some really great country folk in my lifetime; amazing, loyal, good-hearted people. Yet, every time there's some psychos killing and eating folks, it's always hillbillies."

Agent Brennan was looking at him, and it was clear he was unsure of how to answer. "I, uh... I don't know, sir."

"I suppose you wouldn't. You ever been to the country, Brennan? The real country? Deep country like this?"

Agent Brennan shook his head.

"Well, let me explain something to you, son. Out here, you need to be ready for everything. They don't follow the rules or the patterns. They live outside the box and thrive on it. They're jokers and wildcards."

"I understand, sir. I'll keep my guard up and make sure the men are prepared."

Becker nodded and puffed on the cigarette. He looked through the trees in the direction of the house that was too far to see from where they stood. "Make sure everyone stays out of sight and sound until we're ready to go. If they know we're coming, they'll do something crazy. Crazy makes things complicated, Brennan."

"Yes, sir. Got it."

"We need to get up in those trees. Have snipers from every angle. Face the roof and the windows to make sure they can't get the drop on us. You and I are gonna go right up to the front door, but we need to have all exits covered. See if there is a back way to the house, and go the long way around to get to it so they don't spot you and come alive like Frankenstein's monster. How many people are in the house?"

Brennan swallowed hard and looked off. His shoe kicked a rock gently. Becker looked at him with a gaze that should belong to a scolding father. "It's a simple question, son."

Brennan nodded and looked up at him, chewing his lip. "Yes, sir. It's just that... It's not so simple."

"Why not?"

Brennan cleared his throat and tugged on his shirt collar. "Well, there's the grandmother, the mother, and three kids, but folks say there's ghosts in there, the father, the fourth child, the town reverend, and the people they um...ate."

"Holy fuck," Becker said, rubbing at his face like he was trying to wipe it off his skull. "There's no way I'm ever gonna quit smoking with you people. This isn't the *X-Files*, Brennan. It's the real ass FBI. We take on people, living people. Do you believe in that kind of thing, Brennan?"

"I... I'm actually not sure, sir. I've never seen a ghost if that's what you mean, but my mom has this medium she talks to, and he's scarily accurate."

"Christ. Should we bring him in on this? We can delay a bit. Call your mom's medium. Ask him if he can come down and talk to the unliving people for us when we storm the place."

"Yes, sir."

Becker threw down his cigarette and smacked himself in the forehead. "For fuck's sake, Brennan. I didn't mean it."

"Oh." He looked over at the still-smoking butt lying in a pile of dry leaves and hurried over to stamp it out. "Sometimes it's hard to tell when you're not being serious, sir. It, uh...sounds the same."

"Yeah, that's how sarcasm works, son. Jesus. So, outside of the ghosts, we have five people in there? What about the local sheriff's department?"

"Correct. Grandma, Mom, daughter Kyle, and the sons, Jacob and Michael. There was a fourth, Nathaniel, but..." He gulped and dabbed at his forehead sweat with a hanky. "Well, I'm never eating stew again. In any case, the locals have already been rounded up. They had a long history of looking the other way, sir. It seems it went even further than that. Officer Harrison had relations with the family, and others even brought them criminals to eat, calling it 'an everybody wins situation.' That's why we need to move soon. It won't be long before the Collins family realizes we're here."

Becker let out a long, drawn exhale. "Well, then, let's fuckin' do it. Go get everyone in position. When we're all set, meet me at the front so we can follow protocol and let them know that they can come along peacefully if they so choose. Then I'm gonna go home and try acupuncture. I heard it helps people quit."

"My dad used hypnosis."

"That's a nice story, Brennan. Why are you still here?"

Brennan coughed and jumped. "Um, right. Sorry. I'll, uh... Yeah. Okay. Got it."

Becker watched the young agent run off, and he shook his head.

Thirty-Three

A Hand Full of Jokers

Agent Brennan swallowed nervously as he gazed upon the house. There was no need for binoculars now as it stood menacingly right through the trees. "Why am I up here with you again, sir?" he asked. "Everyone is in position as you asked, but I don't have a lot of field experience. Shouldn't I be, um...somewhere in the back?"

Becker sighed and shook his head. His eyes remained trained forward on the target. "Why, hell no, Brennan. You're the one who's fucking this chicken. This is your case. You investigated. You gathered the intel. You got your team together. I'm just here to make sure the bastards get caught or killed, and honestly, I don't particularly care which."

"I thought you were here because of rank, sir. I was instructed to follow your orders."

"Well, then, I'm ordering you to shut the fuck up. Listen, how do you think you advance in rank, Brennan? By cracking the big cases, bringing in the baddies, and taking down the crazies. You're going to stand right next to me. We're gonna do this and then I'm gonna debrief and tell them how you excelled and help you get to where you wanna go."

Brennan blinked. "Wow, uh...thank you, sir."

"Don't thank me. If you move up, I can step back and quit smoking. Everybody wins. So let's get this party started."

"Yes, sir."

Agent Brennan watched nervously with ever-fidgeting hands as his superior agent stepped forward into the open and raised a megaphone to his lips. "Matty May Collins! This is Agent Becker with the FBI. I need you to gather your family and come out unarmed with your hands high. Fun time is over! We've got the house surrounded, and I know you've got your grandkids in there. We've been given permission to use deadly force if you don't comply, and I know you don't want to see anything happen to your grandbabies."

"Shows how much you fuckin' know!" a grizzled old voice shouted back from behind a curtained window. "I watched my son-in-law kill the fuck out of my grandson, and then I ate that fat fucker."

Brennan looked fearfully at Becker. "I think she's telling the truth, sir."

"Yeah, I figured that. Signal one of the boys to take her out. She's the ring leader. Without her, Misty and the kids might surrender."

"Yes, sir."

Brennan stepped off between two trees and spoke quietly into his radio. A moment later, there was a crack as the shot was taken. Becker raised his palms as if to say, *What the fuck?*

Brennan shook his head. "I don't know, sir. Did he...miss?"

When gunfire came their way from the very same window of the house, Becker ducked behind a tree and said, "It sure as hell seems like it."

Then a large shape came careening toward them. They both stared in disbelief as the FBI sniper landed in the dirt, broken like an overused doll. There was a man on top of him who had ridden him down to the ground, but he was all wrong. The man was all one color, including his hair, eyes, and clothes. He was an odd shade of blue. His genitals were exposed, and he stared at them with madness in his gaze as he face-fucked the dead agent, his girthy ghostly appendage sliding in and out of the dead man's frozen scream.

"Sir," Brennan said quietly, "I think that's Frank... The father."

Becker said nothing. He knew why the agent missed his shot at Matty May, but he couldn't make sense out of it. His instincts told him to act, and Brennan watched as he pointed the megaphone right at the apparition and screamed as loud as he could. The ghost blew apart into a million tiny particles like blue confetti drifting through the air after an 'It's a boy!' celebration.

"Is it dead?"

"I don't know, sir."

"Aren't you supposed to be the one who believes in this stuff? You're the Mulder to my Scully, right? So what do we do if it comes back?"

Brennan only shook his head. "Maybe our phones? I've heard camera flashes can dissolve them. But it's all conjecture, sir. I just read things on the internet."

"Fuckin' fantastic." Becker pulled a cigarette out and lit it in a hurry, immediately taking a long drag from the filter. "I can't believe I'm going to say this." He grabbed the radio from Brennan's hands, and the younger agent was left staring at his empty hands in surprise. "Take the house. Anyone you see, you take the shot. Take these fuckin' freaks out, and...watch out for ghosts."

He slammed the radio back into Brennan's hands. "Sir?"

"Shut it."

"Yes, sir."

Gunfire broke out. Windows shattered. Wood chipped and scattered. People were screaming. No more agents were raped by the dead that they could see. Brennan waved the team behind him to advance.

"Go with them," Becker told him.

"Sir?"

"I already told you, it's your show, Slim Shady."

"The album was actually called *The Eminem Show*, sir."

"Just fucking go!"

"Yes, sir."

Brennan was trembling with nerves, but he led the agents who were far more protected in full gear toward the front door. When they reached it, it was already littered with holes. Still, he took a position beside the hinges and raised his gun. He nodded to the point man behind him, who moved past him and kicked the door in.

The moment the door flew open, a shotgun blast sent the agent careening backward. Brennan knew he would survive. He was wearing a vest, but his ribs were probably broken. He swiveled around the door and fired three shots into the chest of Michael Collins, who was far less protected, and collapsed with blood running from his sneering mouth. His chest still rose and fell, but it wouldn't for much longer without medical attention.

When he looked to the right, he saw what looked like a priest. He was holding his hands up in surrender. "I'm not part of the violence. I never was. I'm just here for the dick," he said.

Brennan simply blinked. The holy man was the same odd blue as Frank. He was already dead. "Okay," the agent said quietly.

"Sir?" one of the men behind him said.

"Advance," Brennan told them. "Find the others. Try to take them alive if you can, but if you can't, do what you have to."

"Yes, sir."

He watched as the men poured past him into the house, splitting and going all directions like scurrying roaches. He felt his own limbs trembling less as he went into crisis mode and his nerves steadied themselves.

He heard shouts and a volley of gunfire, and to his own surprise, he hurried in that direction. "What the fuck?" he shouted when he entered the kitchen. It wasn't lost on him that he sounded more like Becker than himself.

The agent stood against the counter, a pot of stew boiling under buzzing flies on the stovetop behind him. Frank's ghost was on his knees sucking the agent's dick. The agent looked at Brennan with a horrified expression. "I don't know, sir. He just appeared and started...ahhh...I uh...fuck...ohhh...I tried to shoot him, but the bullets went right through...oh god."

Brennan holstered his gun and drew his phone. It was time to put the internet to the test. He opened his camera, turned the flash on, and started snapping photos in the felating man's face.

Frank disappeared in a blink, and with no tonsils to pinball off of, the agent's semen became a case of friendly fire. Agent Brennan looked first at the too-thick glob running down his shirt and then at his phone and saw the ghostly man frozen in a picture, staring at him angrily. He wanted to delete it, but was afraid it would return

Frank to the room. Instead, he shoved his phone back in his pocket and looked at the agent's wet, leaking erection. "Put that away and close your pants," he said. "And for God's sake, drink some water. Like fucking ricotta you're shooting. Christ."

"Yes, sir," the agent answered with flushed cheeks as he hurried to zip himself. Brennan moved past him, deeper into the house. When he reached the dining room, the table was set. There were slabs of human meat on the plates, some still containing fingers or toes. He hated how delicious it smelled.

A scream drew his attention, and he spun around. The mother, Misty, was charging him with a butcher knife. There were four loud pops, and she collapsed before she reached him, her face now resembling the meat on the plates. Brennan looked at the agent who had taken her down and nodded his thanks.

He reached the back door and saw what had to be scraps on a pan beside a mop sink. There were genitals and eyeballs among the undecipherable things in the pile. His cheeks puffed, but he forced the bile back down his burning esophagus. He did a thorough check of the room despite how badly he wanted to leave it, opening all the cabinets. When it came up empty, he sighed with relief. Then one of the dicks on the rusty pan started to move. Brennan gasped and stared at it.

It flopped over the metal edge of the tray and onto the floor with a wet slap, and a mouse looked at him, a testicle clutched in its tiny hands. It stared back at him fearlessly as it began to gnaw at the ball with its big teeth. Brennan dry-heaved and quickly left.

"Agent Brennan!" someone shouted.

He hurried in the direction of the shouts, drawing his gun as he went. It led him to one of the bedrooms, where he found Kyle Collins standing naked before two agents. One of her hands was holding a grenade with the pin removed, and the other hand was furiously attacking her clit.

"What the fuck is wrong with you people?" he asked as he stood in the doorway.

"Mmmm, I'm gonna let go and blow the fuck out of all of us if these two don't start blowing each other," she moaned.

Brennan may not have had a lot of field work, but he was one of the fastest and most accurate on the shooting range, and he flipped his gun up and fired, driving her eyeball into her brain and the new concoction out the back of her skull to decorate the wall behind her. One of the agents dove forward and caught the grenade as it came free from her hand. He squeezed the trigger to keep it from blowing, and the man who had been beside him a moment ago sighed with relief. The agent who caught the grenade turned and stared at Brennan. "You could have killed us!" he snapped.

"She would have as soon as she hit her climax if you didn't do as she commanded. It was take her by surprise or let her blow us to hell. I've studied these people," Brennan said, surprised by his own confidence.

"What if I hadn't been fast enough? What if I didn't get it?"

"Then we wouldn't be having this argument, would we?" Brennan asked, moving further down the hall and leaving them in the room.

"What the fuck do I do with it if I can't find the pin?" the agent called behind him.

"I would probably throw it somewhere far away," he called back.

He saw the boy, Jacob, at the end of the hall, glaring at him and clutching a blade like nothing he'd seen before. It looked like a relic, something wicked that had been used in ritual sacrifices somewhere when the world was new.

"Remy and I are going to carve you to pieces for what you've done to my family," Jacob snarled.

"We both know that's not how this is going to go," Brennan told him, raising his gun. "You don't have to die. Drop the knife and we'll take you in."

"Fuck you, pig!"

Somewhere in the distance, an explosion sounded. The house shook. Jacob seized the moment and charged. Brennan spun away from that wicked blade and struck out with his gun, smacking the boy in the bridge of his nose. Blood gushed like a broken faucet from his face, and he stumbled backward.

Brennan swept his legs out from under him, then stomped on his wrist when he hit the ground. The boy cried out in agony as the blade fell from his grip. "This isn't over. You'll die before it's all said and done!"

The agent was staring right at the boy's face. He hadn't spoken, but Brennan had heard the voice clear as day. He looked around and saw no one else. His eyes caught the glinting steel of the blade on the ground, and he had the strangest feeling that the weapon was staring back at him.

Then the agents from the other room rushed in and cuffed the injured boy.

"At least we managed to take one of them alive," Brennan said. He pulled an evidence bag from his coat and bent to pick up the boy's knife with a gloved hand. Then he bagged and tagged it and slid it into his coat. "We still have to find the grandmother," he said.

His radio buzzed. "Go," he said into it.

"Sir, we've cleared the house. Somehow, the grandmother got past us. She's not in here."

As if on cue, a scream sounded from outside. Brennan had never run so fast. He barreled through the front door and down the drive toward the trees. Becker was flat on his back, the megaphone beside him. Grandma Matty May was kneeling beside him, chewing on his intestines. Her face was wet and red, and she glared at Brennan as he came running. She was topless, and her sagging, wrinkled tits were dipped into the dying man's opened body. She rose when she saw Brennan coming, ripping her blood-soaked nipples from the hole in Becker's body. She hissed like a demon, and Brennan put the first bullet through her sharpened yellow teeth, breaking them like ice and ripping through the back of her mouth, sending a clump of wet hair to stick to the tree behind her. She still rose, Becker's intestines in her red-painted hands. She started to run at Brennan; he stopped running and planted his feet firmly in the dusty dirt of the drive. He stood perfectly still as she came and sent his next bullet ripping between her eyes. It took her off her feet, and she hit the ground in a clump.

Brennan didn't check to see if she was dead. He ran again, jumping her body and sliding through the dirt, coming to a stop beside Becker. The superior agent coughed and sprayed blood over Brennan's face. "Bitch got the jump on me," he said. "Always fucking hillbillies."

"Hold on, I'm gonna get you help," Brennan cried as he stared into the open cavern of the man's torso at his chewed-up organs."

"It's too late for that." Becker coughed again. "Guess you'll have to get that promotion without me, but it shouldn't be a problem now."

Brennan said nothing. He didn't know what to say. He just clutched the man's red-speckled hand. "Guess, I finally quit smoking," Becker said with another cough and spray of red that made Brennan grimace and wipe at his face. When he looked back at the man, he was gone.

"Shit." Brennan sighed. He dug out Becker's cigarette pack and lighter. Then he stood, put one between his lips, and lit it. He immediately started coughing.

"Just wait for what's coming next," that strange voice said again. Brennan eyed his jacket and realized the sound was coming from his pocket. "It's me and you now," it said. "I am your destiny."

"What the fuck?"

Thirty-Four

The Beginning

Phillip Brennan sat at his kitchen table, staring into his beer bottle and wondering how everything had gone so wrong. It had been seven days since the raid on the Collins's place, and he still couldn't make sense out of it.

Agent Becker thought he'd get a promotion. Now, Becker was dead, and Phillip was on leave. The way things went, even if he passed the psych eval. to return to work, he would be lucky to ever see the field again. All the work he put in, the months of investigation and intelligence gathering, assembling his team, and securing the most successful field agent still working to lead it, it seemed like he had all his ducks in a row. This should have been it for his career. Even Becker thought so.

Then the grandma ate Becker, the knife in his pocket started talking to him, but apparently nobody else could hear it, and when he tried to give a full statement when being debriefed and mentioned the ghost that had killed the sniper, a good man named Larry Paulson, everything fell apart.

Even when some of the other men corroborated his story, others retold the hand grenade incident, and they blamed him for losing his senior agent being as it was 'his show.'

Now he was home, dealing with mandatory therapy and wondering what job he would even come back to. It was a fucking mess. He sighed and leaned back, polishing off the rest of his beer. Then he tossed it into the trash can and went into the living room, where he stopped before his corner caddy shelf. On top was a photo of his mother and her ashes. On the bottom was a stack of photo albums. In the middle, though, was a plastic stand, and on it stood that bizarre knife Jacob Collins had rushed him with.

Phillip should have given it over, had the damn thing put into evidence with everything else, but he couldn't bring himself to. At first, he'd forgotten all about it as it had gone quiet in his pocket, but then everything had gone south, and he was being sent home without his badge or gun, and he knew his career might very well have ended. By the time he remembered the bizarre blade, he knew he couldn't turn it over. There was a mystery to that thing, and if he wasn't going to be a detective with the FBI anymore, then it very well could be the last mystery he ever got to solve. He had to do something.

He looked at the thing now. "How did you end up with the Collins family?" he asked.

"I was a gift," it said smugly.

He hated the knife as much as he was fascinated by it, but even still, he couldn't argue with its answer. It probably had been a gift. Maybe one of them was lucky enough to find it or to buy it off an antiques dealer or something. They probably had no idea what they were bringing home and just thought it looked cool.

"How come no one else can hear you?"

"I don't know, Phillip boy. Maybe they're not crazy."

Phillip shook his head as he pulled out a cigarette and lit it. When he blew smoke out between his teeth, he said, "No. Bullshit. Becker didn't believe in ghosts, and he stood right beside me and watched one face-fuck Larry Paulson. I know I'm not crazy. Could Jacob hear you?"

"I don't know. Why don't you ask him? Afraid he won't want to talk to you after you murdered the rest of his family?"

He wanted to fire off a retort, but reminded himself that he was talking to an inanimate object and if he allowed himself to argue with it and let it get under his skin, then he probably was as crazy as it accused him of being; as crazy as the FBI saw him, too. Maybe he should go talk to Jacob, he thought. He still had enough pull to get in there for a few minutes, but it could end up as another strike against him later when he was trying to get his job back.

"How many people did you kill while taking residence at the Collins's house?"

"Knives don't kill people, Phillip. People kill people."

"Aargh. Fuck you," Phillip snapped. He stubbed his cigarette out in a ceramic ashtray positioned beside the knife on the same shelf and then headed back to the kitchen for another beer. He'd made that ashtray as a kid, for his mother, who later died of lung cancer. Just another person's death he'd accidentally had a hand in. "Fuck."

He grabbed his new beer, popped the top, and sat at the table. In the relative silence of the place outside of his own troubled thoughts and the yammering of the cursed blade on his shelf, the sudden ringing of his phone made him jump in his seat and knock his drink over. Instead of answering the phone, he just stared at the foamy liquid rolling over the edge of his table onto his floor like white water rapids down a waterfall. He sighed heavily.

When the phone didn't stop, Phillip grabbed it to see who it was. Not many people bothered to stay in touch, and the ones who did usually texted. Carol. He sighed again and decided to answer as the spilling beer continued its descent.

"Hey," he said, his voice displaying his fatigue.

"I just wanted to check on you. I'm gonna be in the area if you need anything."

"A job?" he said with a laugh.

"Hey, come on. You haven't been fired, bud. If you were them, you would order a shrink and psych eval. too, and you know it."

"I know. That's why I don't have much hope."

"Just play by the rules, and Dr. Meyers will clear you. Then you'll come back and put it all behind you."

"In what position, though? I thought this was my break, Carol."

"How do you know it wasn't? Maybe when you're cleared, they'll actually start the *X-Files* and put you at the head of it."

"Is that the type of thing going around the office?"

"No. I promise. That's all just me trying to make things lighter. In fact, Tommy Zozorro said he saw a ghost at that house, swears by it."

"And he's not on leave?"

"He was, Phillip. He just got back. That's what I'm saying. Just go to your appointment, man."

"I appreciate the concern, but I'll be alright."

"You'll be a pain in my ass. We've been friends since Quantico. You don't get to see a couple of ghosts and bail on me."

Phillip found himself laughing for real. He was happy to know he still could. "You hungry?" he asked.

"Starving. You're buying. When you run out of money, you'll have to jump through the hoops and come back to work."

He shook his head and chuckled. "Fine. Meet me at the park in fifteen."

"Be there in ten."

"I would expect no less. I'll be there in twenty."

"I know."

Phillip smiled as he hung up the phone. He felt genuinely better and stood to grab a towel from the handle of the oven. Then he got to work cleaning up the beer that was forming quite a puddle on the kitchen tiles. He looked over and his eyes caught sight of the knife on his shelf.

"Who was that? She sounds nice. You should kill her," the knife said.

"Pssh. Yeah, kill one of the few people I've got left. Is that the type of thing you told Jacob? How much of what that family did did you set in motion?"

"You sure have a lot of questions."

"Yeah, because you don't fucking answer any." When the knife went quiet, Phillip scoffed and stood, throwing the sopping towel into the sink for him to deal with later. He didn't have a packed schedule. There would be plenty of time.

As he crossed the living room heading for the front door, he glanced over at the knife again. "Who are you anyway?"

"Name's Remy. Nice to officially meet. Now we can start bonding."

Phillip frowned and hurried out of his apartment like it were an unsafe place. The knife was an inanimate object, even if it was a chatty one, so why did he feel like there was a killer behind him, watching him go?

Thirty-Five

Do You Wanna Meet Him?

Phillip strolled to the park, late as expected, sipping on a steaming cup of coffee. He waved to Carol, who was already sitting comfortably on a bench, deep in a book with her bag beside her and a pastry wrapper on her lap. He smirked as he approached. "Still getting the pre-lunch croissant, huh?"

"I pregame for everything, bruh. Before my first date with my wife, I went and fucked a dude just to get me hankering for an actual orgasm."

Phillip laughed his ass off. It felt good. "You're definitely one of a kind."

"Uh oh, that's what that guy said after leaving me wholly unsatisfied, like I knew he would. Where are you taking me for lunch? It's not fast food, is it? I can't eat that crap."

Phillip shook his head. With a smile, he said, "What if the fast food is just a pregame for the steakhouse?"

"Then it sounds like we'll need to make a pit stop at a shit spot."

"Maybe we can stop at my place and you can meet Remy."

Her left eyebrow jumped toward her hairline. "Remy?"

"Oh, yeah. Just the talking knife, who I'm pretty sure has murdered a ton of people. Chatty guy. Bit of a smart ass though."

"And you resent the psych eval.?"

"Just wait 'til you meet him. Make your own assessment of my mental state after."

She smiled. "Alright, I'm game. But first... Feed me, Seymour!"

"Alright. Come on. We are getting burgers, but they won't be fast. Alfonzo makes them with love. They take forever but taste like a million bucks."

"They taste like cocaine?"

"I said a million bucks, not a rolled-up hundred."

Carol stood. "The hundred is just the pregame," she said, slapping him on the back as she passed him and strolled down the path. Phillip shook his head, threw her croissant wrapper in the nearby trash can, and hurried to catch up.

As they sat waiting for their burgers, Carol said, "I should have been with you that day, Phil."

He huffed. "I was worried you were gonna do that. Don't make this about you, please."

She reached across the table and punched him in the arm. It hurt and would probably bruise, but he made sure not to show his discomfort. "I'm not," she said when she sat back. "I'm just saying, I should have been by your side. I should have been there to help when things went south or to back you up and say I saw what you saw when all was said and done."

He sighed. "You're bitter that I didn't pick you for the team."

"I'm not, but why didn't you?"

Phillip stared at her. "Seriously?"

She raised her palms and stared back.

He huffed but nodded. "Alright. Well, I knew if I told you to go one way, you'd go the other and take two people with you. If I said you needed to listen to me, you would laugh in front of everyone. I don't think Becker could have even controlled you. It was my show, and I wanted it to stay my show, and even that grizzled old bastard didn't want to step on my toes. He wanted me to get the credit. I don't think he knew how the dust would settle, though."

"Wow, you're a dick."

"You made me tell you."

"Did I? Did I put a gun to your head? Does your talking knife make people kill?"

"I actually don't know the answer to that."

"You don't know if I put a gun to your head or not?"

"I meant the other part."

Alfonzo came over and brought their burgers with a smile. He set her plate down and went to set Phil's down, but Carol took it. She set it on her booth bench beside her. Alfonzo looked at her with confusion, and she said, "He's an asshole, so I'm gonna eat both."

"Ah! His will be the pregame for your own meal," Alfonzo said with a grin.

Carol pointed at Phillip and gave him a side-eye. "How does everyone know me better than you, and you're supposed to be my best friend?"

Phillip huffed. "Alright. I get it. Can I please have my lunch?"

"Oh, hell no, but you're still buying."

Phillip knew he was pouting like a child on the walk back to his place, but he couldn't help it. He had already been feeling sorry for himself before one of his only friends ate his lunch. "I can't believe you actually made me pay for the food you forced me to watch you eat."

"Hey, I bought you lunch on the way back here."

"You got me a pretzel."

"Ungrateful shit."

"So you coming up?"

"Well, I don't suppose you'd bring Remy down?"

"I... No. I don't like to touch it. I...don't trust it."

Carol smirked and started to sing the *X-Files* music.

"There's something wrong with that thing for real. It came from the Collins house, but I think it was around long before that."

"Speaking of coming and the Collins house, do you think ghost dad can jizz? Is there like phantom cum that flies out of his transparent pecker? Can you not see anything but feel the sudden wetness of his gush?"

"I don't fucking know, Carol. You joke, but the image of that is going to be burned into my mind forever."

"I wish I were joking. This is shit I really wanna know."

"Why?" he asked, fishing his keys out when they reached his building. "You think ghost guys would be any less unsatisfying?"

"I mean, that *is* the question, isn't it?"

He just shook his head and led her up. When he opened his apartment door, Phillip realized he felt suddenly apprehensive. He felt like he was walking into a lion's den. Why would that one stupid object make him feel this way about his own home?

"Beer me," she said as she fearlessly walked around him into the place.

"I thought you said you had plans to go drinking with Abby after this."

"Pregame, mutherfucker, shit. And you thought I wouldn't listen."

"I love you, but I also hate you," he said as he went to the fridge.

"Shit, don't get me horny. I'm married now. That's when men can actually fuck. Conflicting emotions make for great sex."

He came back and put a beer in her hand. She was already standing in his living room, staring at Remy. "Is it talking to you?" he asked warily.

"The knife? No. It's just sitting there looking pretty. Thing looks old, Phil, really old."

"I know. That's what I'm saying. How many people did that thing kill before it even found its way to the Collins house?"

"Do you really think he talks to you?"

"I don't know that it's a him. The name is unisex, and the voice doesn't betray any kind of gender."

"So, that's a yes, then."

"Let me fuck her," Remy said. I'll fuck her *real* good."

"Yeah, I don't think so," Phillip told it.

"You don't think what?" she asked, looking over.

"You actually can't hear it, can you?"

"The knife?"

"Yes. It was... Never mind. You want to sit on the couch and catch up a bit?"

"Well, no, you fucking nutball. I want to understand this knife deal."

"I do too, Carol, but I don't know if it can be understood. I need to find out where it came from, who the spirit trapped inside is, and what to do about it."

Carol looked at him with childlike excitement, her eyes wide. "Is that your theory? That there's a spirit trapped inside the blade? Like Jack the Ripper or some shit?"

"I don't know, but I can't think of any other reason it would have a name and a voice."

"You paranormal nerds always crack me up," Remy said. "How about the guy who forged me gave me a name? Some things are just that simple."

"Who was it?" Phillip asked. "Who forged you?"

"I'm tired of all this talking. It's exhausting. Can I please stab someone now? Cut at least? Please?"

Carol's excitement intensified. "Did it just say something to you? What did it say? Ask it why the fuck I can't hear it? That's rude. Is it a man thing? Is this just another way for a man to fuck me?"

"Tell her I'm not a man, I'm a knife, but she can still stroke me if she wants to."

"Tell her yourself," Phillip snapped.

"Tell her what? Tell me what? What?"

"Forget it," Phillip told her. "I took photos of it and searched the internet too. Came up empty. I went to the library. I found nothing."

"Because the answer is not in words," Remy said. "The answer is in blood."

Before Phillip could respond, Carol reached over and picked the knife up. He gasped as he watched. He was careful to keep it bagged and then not to touch it when he unbagged it. He had no idea what would happen upon skin contact. "Are you okay?" he asked her.

She held the blade out before her and slashed at the air like a swashbuckler. "You really think this blade has killed people?"

"It tried to kill me."

"Oh come on, no I didn't. Jacob tried to kill you. I was just brought along for the ride. I knew that kid was temporary. You and I were always meant to be, big boy."

"I wish it would talk to me so I could know that my bestie isn't a psychopath," Carol said with a pout of her own.

"Please just put it down. Put it back. Come on. Please."

Carol's eyes widened, then, like she heard something, but that couldn't be because Phillip hadn't heard anything. "Holy shit," she said.

He looked at her with fear in his gaze. "Is it...talking?"

"Don't you hear it? You've been listening to it the whole time."

"I know...but, no...I didn't hear anything."

"Oh hell, you are suave, aren't you?" she said, looking at the blade in her hand. "I guess Remy can pick and choose who can hear it at any time."

"I don't like that. Please put it down. You've heard it now. Let's go somewhere away from the knife and talk about it."

"Heard it? I'm still hearing it. Remy has a lot to say, Phil. You were right. They've been around a very long time, and they've seen so much. It's amazing to hear. I have to know more. Someone needs to write it down."

"Okay. Let's do that. But for now, let's put it away."

"I can't do that."

"What the fuck does that mean, Carol? Just put it down." He was panicking now, backing away from her. He wished he could hear what Remy was saying to her. Not knowing, but knowing it was talking, was making him crazy.

"I'm going to take Remy with me," she said forcefully. "Don't try to stop me. This is important."

"What? No," Phillip snapped.

"I have to do this."

"You don't have to do shit."

"Step back, Phil."

"Fuck you. No."

That's when she lunged at him with the knife. He jumped back but moved around to block the door. He couldn't let her out of the apartment with that thing. He knew in his gut that people would die. Carol wasn't herself. He didn't know what Remy had said to influence her, but whatever it was, it worked.

She slashed at him in a wild arc.

"Carol, stop this! You have to stop!" he cried, his eyes darting back and forth, watching her for sudden movements. She slashed at him again. He moved out of the way, but the blade still tore through his sleeve and nicked his arm. He wished in that moment that he hadn't been made to turn in his gun. If he had it, he could have hit her somewhere nonvital, taken her down, and gotten that damn thing away from her.

"I don't want to kill you," she said as she lashed at him. "I love you, you know that, and I don't love anything with a penis. So please get out of my way."

"Why?!" he screamed. "Why not just put the damn thing down? Why not stop this?"

"I can't, goddammit. This is bigger than you and me, Phil. You have to move."

He shook his head and stood his ground. "No."

A knock sounded at the door, and he instinctively turned to look. He was hit from behind, and as he fell to the ground, he watched Carol charge past him toward the door with Remy in hand. "No!" he cried, reaching toward them.

She ripped the door open, grabbed his neighbor, Mr. Rowland, from the apartment across the way by his shirt, and dragged him wide-eyed into the room, slamming the door behind him. The man looked terrified. He stared at Phillip, who was making his way back to his feet. "I just needed milk for Mr. Whiskerfluff. What is this?"

"Carol, let him go," Phillip barked.

She laughed. It sounded strange. He'd heard her laugh a million times over the years, and it never sounded like that. He looked behind him at the shelf with his mother's ashes. When he looked back, she had slit Mr. Rowland's throat so he couldn't scream for help. Still, he gurgled and choked. Blood was running like a river down his shirt. She immediately began hacking, stabbing, and slashing at him as he fell onto the already squishy carpet. Meat flew like wedding day confetti, and blood sprayed all the furniture around. The hungry, maniacal knife seemed to grab onto the organs when it dipped inside the man. Upon its release, it would pull them to the surface, leaving him like a Thanksgiving Day cornucopia of gore. Carol was so occupied helping Remy commit murder that she didn't see or feel Phillip close in. He slammed her across the skull with the ceramic ashtray. She fell beside his dying neighbor.

"Fuck," Phillip snapped.

She tried to rise, madness in her eyes and the knife still in her hand, and he struck her again and again. When she fell, he continued to bring the ashtray down on her head until he knew she wasn't getting back up.

Her skull caved in, and her eye popped out, dangling, rubbing against her furiously twisted lips. Bits of skull and brain clung to the ashtray like Velcro. Then he dropped it into the ever-growing lake of crimson taking over his living room, and he fell to his knees with his head in his hands.

"FUCK!"

Thirty-Six

What the Fuck am I Supposed to do Now, Huh?

Phillip Brennan sat on his knees in his living room, holding his head and repeating the "F" word over and over.

"Christ, you're dramatic," Remy said.

Phillip snarled and glared at the knife that had now fallen from Carol's limp hand and lay on the cushiony fabric of the blood-soaked rug. "Oh, now you want to talk to me again?"

"Well, I kinda have to. You *killed* her."

"You made me! You made this happen!"

The damn thing sighed. "Did I? Did I put a gun to your head? Does your talking knife make you kill people?" Remy laughed.

Phillip wanted to burn the thing, to melt it down to nothing, but his gut told him it wouldn't be that simple. The blade didn't make it this long for no reason. Whatever it was forged from, it would continue. "This is a fucking mess," he said weakly, tears rolling from his eyes. "What am I supposed to do?"

"Well, I'd think that much would be obvious, Phil."

He wiped his wet nose with the back of his hand, smearing blood on his face, unsure of whose it was. "Enlighten me."

"Well, you already know if you call it in, no one will believe you. If they were going to believe you, you wouldn't be home right now, scheduled to talk to a psychiatrist tomorrow. She was a decorated agent, still working. You already got Becker killed. This will seal your career coffin forever."

"I hate you."

"Yeah, whatever. Cry me a river. Anyway, you're gonna have to cut her up, both of 'em, and dispose of the bodies. You gotta get this rug cleaned up too before it starts dripping into the apartment below. If you go to prison, it will really complicate things for me."

"You think I'm worried about you? You ruined my life. Fuck off."

"Sheesh. You are really quick to pass the buck, aren't you, Phillip boy? Did I give an ashtray to your mom and help her smoke more? No. You did that. Did I plan a raid on the Collins house and pick the team of people? No, you did that. You put the people who died that day in that spot. You did. Did I take that same hand-crafted ashtray and bash your best friend's skull in? Nope. You did. Did I make you keep the knife instead of turning it over to evidence?

Nope again. Noperoo, Mister Magoo. You fucking did. Did I have photographic proof of a ghost on my phone and show no one because 'I just didn't think of it in the moment'? Noperooni. So quit your goddamn crying and man-up or hand me to someone with an actual worthy pair of balls or better yet, a vulva since women know how to get shit done."

Phillip just blinked and stared at the talking blade. He couldn't say anything back. What could he say? As much as he hated to admit it, Remy was right about everything. He had fucked everything up and gotten a lot of people killed. Why hadn't he shown the picture of Frank to the higher-ups? It was his frozen spirit. He knew the answer. He was afraid of it. He was spooked that Frank still had power from that still-frame and would do something to him or someone else, and it would wind up his fault. A lot of good that did.

"Hey, I don't have any hands, fuck weasel. You gotta start cleaning this shit up. Just grab me. I can cut right through bone. I've done it a ton of times. I'm useful, Phillip. Let's get a move on."

"No."

"No?"

"No. If I pick you up, I'm just going to slit my own throat and be done with this."

"Christ. Just grow your bangs over one eye and buy a pair of skinny jeans, why don't you? You know what'll happen if you off yourself, Captain Shriveled Nuts. When someone finds this scene and plasters all over the world that you were a psycho serial murderer, I'll get picked up and go with someone else and live happily ever after, just like I always do."

Phillip's lip twitched. He stared at the blade and roared in anger.

"Keep it down unless you want someone else at the door who you'll have to kill."

"I'm not killing anyone."

"Else?"

"Shut up."

Phillip got to his feet and started pacing. He didn't know what to do. Remy was right. He had to take the knife somewhere, get rid of it, and make sure it didn't cause any more havoc. He no longer cared about the mystery, the origin, the story. He just cared that no one else died. To make sure the knife was properly disposed of, he had to clean this up. He could turn himself in after the knife was gone, but if people started coming for him before that, he could get caught, and Remy could end up in someone else's hands, and it could keep the cycle of death going. He couldn't allow that.

With a sigh and fresh tears rolling down his cheeks, Phillip picked up Carol and Mr. Rowland and dragged them to the bath-tub. He cringed at the uncompromising position they landed in with Mr. Rowland's head between Carol's legs and his crotch in her face. Her hanging eyeball rested on the dead man's anus and stared back at Phillip accusingly. "I'm sorry," he moaned, hurrying from the room.

"I'm sorry," Remy mocked. He gave the knife a showing of his middle finger and grabbed supplies from under the sink to clean the carpet. It was going to take more than paper towels. He got the foaming carpet cleaner and sprayed it everywhere, then went over it with the wet vac. He was hard at work and didn't hear the knocking at first, but when he stopped the vacuum to wipe sweat from his brow, he heard the assault on his door. *No,* he thought. *It's too soon.*

He looked down at himself and realized his clothes were completely covered in bright red evidence. "Fuck," he grumbled, running into his bedroom as the knocking continued.

"Phil, are you in there?" an older female voice crooned. "Phillip Brennan!"

Christ. It was old Donna from next door. What the hell did she want? He hadn't answered. Why didn't she just go away?

He ripped his bloody clothes off and threw them in the bathtub with the bodies. Then grabbed a washcloth and did a quick wash of his arms, neck, and face. He tied a towel around his waist for dramatic effect and ran to the door. When he ripped it open, Donna looked at him like he was shoving his dick in her face and demanding she suck it. She looked downright repulsed and offended. Then she was moving side to side on her tippytoes, trying to see past him. He was ready to scream, "What the hell do you want?" but he bit it back.

"Hey," he said instead. "Not a great moment. What's up?"

"Have you seen Roland?" she asked.

"You mean Rowland? Mr. Rowland? From across the hall?"

She met his eyes then, her stare hard. "Yes. Roland Rowland. He was looking for milk for my cat because I ran out, and I haven't seen him come back. Mr. Whiskerfluff is thirsty."

Shit. He'd forgotten that Mr. Whiskerfluff wasn't Mr. Rowland's cat. He couldn't keep up with that shit. But before he could comment on that, he word vomited his first thought. "Mr. Rowland's name was Roland? Roland Rowland? Seriously?"

"Why did you say 'was'?" she asked, scrutinizing him.

"Just misspoke. Slip of the tongue."

"Did something happen to Roland?"

He shrugged. "I don't know. I haven't seen him."

"Oh, just fucking kill the bitch already," Remy shouted from behind him.

"Listen, Donna... I have to get back in the shower. Unless you want to come get my back for me, this conversation is going to have to be over."

She looked appalled and struck out, slapping him across the face. He didn't expect her to go that far and blinked in shock. "You're disgusting," she said.

"She hit you! Fucking gut the bitch. Come on!" Remy called to him.

"I hope you find Mr. Rowland," Phillip said, stepping back and shutting the door.

"Well, that was a missed opportunity," Remy said. "Can we go cut some people up now? I hope you have trash bags."

"Will you just shut the fuck up?!" Phillip had lost it. He couldn't take listening to that damn thing anymore. He regretted screaming immediately, though, when the knocking returned.

Donna was shouting through the door. "Who are you yelling at in there? It's not my Roland, is it? Is he in there? I need milk for Mr. Whiskerfluff!"

Remy laughed. "Come on, Phillip. You know you want to. We can just add her to the pile. Easy peasy."

"I'm not going away until I see who's in there with you. I already know you're a pervert! You better not try to do gross things to that nice Mr. Rowland!"

Phillip growled. He believed her. She wasn't going to go away. It would be another life gone, but it would prevent how many more. If he got caught when he still had the knife, so many others would die. He snatched Remy off the ground, marched back to the front door, yanked it open, and said, "I really wish you would have just gone home, Donna."

She eyed the knife in his hand. "What is that? What are you doing? Did you hurt Roland?"

He huffed and yanked her by her hair into the apartment, kicking the door shut once she was inside. "Let me go! Rape! Rape!" she screamed.

"What the fuck?" Phillip snapped. "I'm not going to rape you."

"Oh my god. Are you one of those? Did you rape Roland?"

"Holy shit, she's a piece of work. Please just shut her up already," Remy groaned in his hand. Phillip sighed and slashed the blade across her mouth. It split her cheek to cheek, and she looked like the Joker with an old lady beehive hairdo. He slashed again, but she was pulling away, and the knife plunged into the side of her face. Her dentures came loose and slid out of the hole onto the floor.

"Holy fuck, that was gnarly," Remy said. "You're a natural."

"Shut up," Phillip commanded.

"I'm thorry," Donna cried without her teeth in her mutilated mouth. She must have thought he was talking to her. Fuck, what a mess.

He tried to give the finishing blow and drive Remy right into the side of her head again, but she yanked backward, and the knife drove straight into her ear. Phillip gasped. When he pulled the knife back to strike again, the ear detached from her head and came with it. He stared at it with wide, horrified eyes.

"Say something," Remy joked. "See if I can hear you better."

Phillip was still staring at the ear on the knife when he realized Donna was trying to attack him. He spun to face her as she was coming with a knobby-knuckled haymaker. His mouth fell open, but her old fist never connected. She slipped on her own dentures, and her legs went out from under her. She fell backward and her head smacked the corner of the coffee table with a wet *thuck!*

"Well, that's disappointing," Remy said. "I still get to cut her up, right?"

"Let's just make it quick," Phillip answered with an exhausted exhale.

Thirty-Seven

Don't Skimp on Trash Bags or Toilet Paper

Phillip thought he would need a bone saw or a hungry pig to get through a dead body, but Remy was right. That knife was born for this, maybe literally. He didn't know who created it or why, but he was sure it wasn't anything good. Still, that blade never seemed to dull. It cut through flesh and bone and just kept on going. What was worse was the moans of ecstasy it made while doing it.

"Come on, huh," he said as he slashed the knife through Roland's hip. "Can we please do this more quietly?"

"Mmmm, fuck no," Remy said. "This is what it's all about, my lame ass friend. Send me in again."

Phillip rolled his eyes and groaned, but he drove the knife into the other thigh, removing it. The blade screamed in orgasmic frenzy. Phillip grumbled about being in the world's worst porn, and Remy laughed. "Come on, Phillip boy. Live a little."

"I'll pass. Carol meant a lot to me, you prick."

"Then you shouldn't have killed her, you little crybaby bitch."

Phillip's lip twitched, but he bit back his retort and started shoveling the already cut pieces into the thick black trash bags he got from the dollar store. They were labeled heavy duty, so he was hoping that was true.

"Are you not gonna eat that?" Remy said, sounding disappointed.

"What? Jesus. No."

"Well, you're missing out. I've been making fine cuts of meat like that for plenty of mouths, Phillip. Have a taste."

"Fuck off. Just shut up and cut."

"Weeeeeee!" Remy screamed like a child on a swing as it was driven in to remove Carol's tits. They slid right off and slid down into the tub. Phillip silently apologized to her wife, who would never get to see or feel or taste them again. He reached into the tub and fished them out to throw them into the trash bag.

"Don't forget the mouthy chick from next door. We gotta dice her up too," Remy said.

Phillip was exhausted and sick of this knife. He was sick of this life. He grabbed some toilet paper off the roll nearby and tried to wipe some blood splatter from his face. His finger pushed through the paper, and he poked himself in the eye. Crying out, he dropped the paper on the floor. Remy was laughing at him, and it made him want to scream and burn the world.

"Hey, that's your fault too," Remy told him. "You never skimp on TP, champ, unless of course, you like fingering assholes. No judgment here. I love sticking my tip in an asshole now and then."

"I really do wish I didn't kill Carol because when she had you, that was the only time you've been quiet since I met you."

"Stop crying and let's keep the blood flying!" Remy said.

Phillip sighed, but it did have to be done, so he brought the chatty kathy down in an arc and sliced the ass off his best friend's corpse.

When the bodies were all cut into pieces and stuffed into two giant trash bags, Phillip turned the shower on and stepped in. "Take me with you," Remy said. "I'm so dirty and I want you to make me wet."

Phillip groaned but decided it probably was good to wash the blood off the knife and get rid of the evidence. When they were both clean and shiny, he dressed in fresh blood-free clothes and stashed the knife in the inside pocket of his suit jacket, the same place he had smuggled it in from the Collins's house. He grabbed a trash bag in each hand and made his way to the elevator, which was decorated with an OUT OF ORDER sign that made him curse and laugh simultaneously.

He groaned and grumbled as he strained to drag the impossibly heavy bags of human remains down the stairs. When he got outside, he moaned with tiredness and then made the last part of his journey to the cans at the curb. He lifted one bag up high with a grunt and dropped it inside the can with a clanging bang.

Angelique from the second floor said, "You seen Donna? Her pussy got loose. I tried to grab it, but it hissed at me. Normally, I'm quite good at grabbing pussy."

He hadn't realised she was even there and it took a second for his nerves to settle. "Nope. Sorry," Phillip said, lifting the other bag. He felt it tearing before he saw it and hurried to get it in the can, but the bottom exploded outward, and pieces of people came tumbling out, banging against the cans and scattering everywhere. Phillip turned slowly to look at Angelique, who was frozen in place, staring at him with wide eyes. He cringed in a sort of terrified forced smile and said, "Oh, there she is. You should tell her you found her cat." He punctuated it with a nervous laugh.

Angelique came to life then. "Help!" she screamed, running off down the road.

"Fuck!" Phillip snapped. There was no fixing this one. He just had to get rid of the knife before he got grabbed.

"You really fucked that up," Remy said from his pocket as he took off down the road toward the river. "Damn. TP and trash bags. You never skimp on either. This is why. Some things you pay extra for the name brands, man. You get what you pay for, you know?"

Phillip did his best to ignore Remy and just kept running. He saw the bridge going over the river and thought it was the best chance he had of getting rid of the damn knife before anyone else died. "Oh come on, you're not gonna toss me after everything we've been through together, are you? Can we talk about this?" Remy pleaded.

Phillip still said nothing. He pulled the knife from his pocket and walked to the guardrail at the side of the bridge. He looked over at the water with the wind whipping at his face and hair. He felt like he should probably go into the river too, but he didn't want to be near the knife. He decided he would throw Remy out first, as far as he could throw it. Then he would jump. He couldn't live with himself after everything.

"It doesn't have to end this way," Remy said. "Someone will eventually find me again. They always do. They always will. A fisherman, a diver, an eco-friendly good Samaritan river cleaner—someone. You're just delaying it at best. Why not just find someone to give me to? I make a nice gift. I'm quite beautiful. Come on, you know it. I see the way you look at me. Are you even fucking listening right now? Come on. Fuck!"

Phillip felt in his bones that Remy was probably right, and one day down the line, someone would find the knife and it would all start again, but his hope was that it would be years before that day came. Maybe he couldn't stop the knife from killing and wreaking havoc, but in holding it off as long as possible, he would still be saving lives. He owed the world that much after all the lives he'd helped death claim.

He reached into his pocket and dug out one of Becker's final cigarettes. "Sorry, Mama," he said as he put it between his lips and lit it. He took a big drag and lifted the knife high, prepared to throw it.

"Put the knife down now!" a voice shouted from behind him. Phillip didn't need to look to know it was the police. He knew he couldn't argue or try to reason with them, especially if they saw the body parts scattered all over in front of his apartment building. He moved to throw Remy into the water. It was all he could do to make things right. He had to try.

He heard the *Bang! Bang! Bang!* Before he felt anything.

The knife tumbled from his hand and clattered against the concrete instead of sailing into the ocean, and tears tumbled from his eyes at his failure and what it would mean. He fell hard to his knees and moaned, "Please. You have to get rid of it."

Then he fell onto his face and lay still.

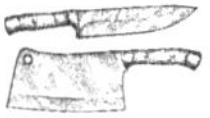

Officer Jordonna moved to the guy to see if he was still alive. "He's gone," she called back to Officer Bercy.

"Shit," Bercy said, walking over. He stopped and looked down at the strange blade on the floor, a foot or so away from where the murderer fell. "You think this is what he did it with?"

"It would make sense why he was trying to get rid of it, if it was," Jordonna said back. "You call this in and I'll bag it up, just in case."

She slipped on a glove and squatted down before the knife with a huge Ziploc bag in her hand. When she grabbed the handle of the knife, she felt something strange, like an electrical surge pulse through her. She almost dropped it. Jordonna stared at the strange weapon. "What the hell is your story?" she asked, not expecting an answer.

"Well, it's a long one if you really want to hear it. Pleasure to meet you, my new friend. My name's Remy. And you are?"

Content Note